PRAISE FOR DAVID HAYNES AND **HEATHENS**

"One of the best young voices in American literature."—*Minneapolis Star Tribune*

"Rich, textured voices . . . make the novel such a treat for lovers of well-drawn characters and well-crafted prose."—*Dallas Morning News*

"These figures are so well drawn you almost smell them, their stories delivered with flawless comic timing and chameleon-like shifting from one character's perspective to the next."—*Scrawl*

"A prose writer of the first order—his firm, biting sentences snap you awake and justify your attention."—*Hungry Mind Review*

"Haynes's artful fiction should appeal to a wide audience."—*Kirkus Reviews*

HEATHENS

A Novel

David Haynes

Delta
Trade Paperbacks

A Delta Book
Published by
Dell Publishing
a division of
Bantam Doubleday Dell Publishing Group, Inc.
1540 Broadway
New York, New York 10036

ISBN: 0-385-31891-X

Reprinted by arrangement with New Rivers Press

Manufactured in the United States of America
Published simultaneously in Canada

November 1997

10 9 8 7 6 5 4 3 2 1

BVG

Acknowledgments

The author thanks the Ragdale Foundation and the Virginia Center for the Creative Arts for the time and space to create this work.

Special thanks to Bill Truesdale for his editorial advice, and to Michelle Woster, Phyllis Jendro, and the rest of the New Rivers team for all of their hard work on my behalf.

"Heathens" originally appeared in a slightly different form in *Other Voices.*

"Busted" originally appeared in a slightly different form in *Glimmer Train Stories* and has been recorded for the National Public Radio Series Selected Shorts.

Contents

Heathens

On a Sunday afternoon in April Marcus Gabriel and his son Ali are trapped in the express lane at the Highland Park Country Lane market. In the middle of preparing a batch of dump cookies as a peace offering to Marcus's mother, Verda, they have run out of sugar. Marcus hates days like this: cool, bugless spring days when every Lutheran in St. Paul starts the car only to drive around aimlessly. The Catholics, too. Outside the grocery the streets are clotted with traffic—much worse than State Fair time. At least at fair time the Lutherans and the Catholics and the farmers stay up by the fairgrounds. Driving the two miles from Tangletown to the supermarket, no less than four drivers courteously yielded the right-of-way to Marcus. "All that niceness," Marcus said to Ali. "That's what causes accidents."

There are six customers in front of them in the ten-items-or-less lane. Marcus has a five pound bag of Domino sugar and six bottles of mandarin orange spring water. Ali carries the Pringles Light BBQ chips and a cellophane package of cashews. The cashews are for the dump cookies.

Marcus nudges Ali. "Go up there and make sure everybody has ten items or less."

Ali reports back that the old woman with the blue rinse has eleven, maybe twelve items.

"Go give her a dirty look," Marcus orders.

"Do it yourself," Ali says. He goes back to reading his skateboard magazine. Ali is twelve. He has walked up and down every aisle with his face stuck in *Freestyle Deluxe* magazine. The potato chips are for him, or at least that is what he would like to believe.

Five minutes later there are still three people in front of them. The other lanes are six or seven people deep—Lutherans with baskets full of nutritious foods. Ali shifts impatiently from one hip to another, sighing loudly.

"If you had roughed up that old lady when I asked you to, we'd be out of here by now," Marcus chides.

Ali is not amused. "If we'd gone to a real grocery store, we'd be home. But, no. Marcus has to go to the Country Lane. This fuckin store don't even have scanners."

"Doesn't," Marcus corrects. "And this is the only store that has mandarin orange spring water on Sundays."

"We could have gone to the fuckin SuperAmerica for that."

Ali uses the word *fuckin* in every other sentence. As a sixth grade teacher Marcus sometimes feels the need to extinguish this behavior. Whenever he remembers to do so, somehow fuckin seems like the correct word. It also seems too much the sort of thing his mother, Verda, would do.

So instead Marcus says, "Well I'm not twelve and I don't know everything. Besides: I always run into my students at SuperAmerica. Shoplifting." Marcus bobs his head around like an owl when he says this. Then he pops the top off the chips and dumps some out to eat, hoping they will make Ali less cranky. Ali's been cranky ever since LaDonna, Ali's mother and Marcus's significant other, was sentenced to thirty days in the Shakopee Women's Detention Center for trying to sell a house on Dayton Avenue that she really didn't own to a cartel of Japanese business men. It would have been fifteen days, but LaDonna waved her arms around claiming to put a hex on the judge. Sometimes LaDonna didn't know when to quit.

"Oh for pity's sake," says the old man in front of them. A lot of old people shop at the Country Lane. Marcus believes they are old Lutherans who have a fear of scanners. This old man is wearing suspenders and a plaid shirt. In one hand he's got a twenty pound turkey and in the other hand he's got a bucket of green stuff.

Ali and Marcus lean around in different directions, nonchalantly trying to get a look at the bucket. The old man gives them suspicious looks. They act innocent, Ali by reading the skateboard magazine, Marcus by reading the headlines of the *Weekly World News*. Another baby born tattooed. Once Marcus had a contest for his sixth graders to see who could write the best headlines. Marcus won by himself anonymously submitting "Storybook Romance Ends as Legless Man Shoots Dwarf Bride." That was an actual headline. You could never make them up as good as the real ones. This was just one of Marcus's many strange assignments. His students couldn't do any of them. Like Ali, most young adolescents nowadays suffered from some kind of warped cynicism. They believed in tattooed babies and in the real love between Whitney Houston and Bobby Brown. They didn't believe in weather forecasts or in anything that happened before 1974.

"What do you suppose is in that bucket?" Ali whispers.

"Irish mashed potatoes," Marcus answers.

Finally Marcus and Ali dump their goods on the conveyor belt. The checkout person hooks a finger over Ali's magazine. "Get that here?" she asks.

Ali recoils and squinches up his face.

"He's deaf and mute," Marcus says. "No one knows where those magazines come from."

Declining a paper bag, they carry their purchases to the Bronco.

"Watch this," Marcus says. He pulls out onto Snelling Avenue. He accelerates to forty and weaves in and out of the Sunday drivers, passing Lutherans on the left, Catholics on the right.

"You drive like a crazy person," Ali says.

"Lime sherbet," Marcus says. Ali nods in agreement. They have already eaten all of the cashews.

Marcus tastes a spoonful of dump cookie batter. He makes Ali taste it too. They both shrug. It's hard to say with dump cookies. A raisin bite tastes sweet, a nut bite doesn't. Marcus dumps in more sugar. That's how you make dump cookies—dump in a little of this, dump in a little of that.

Dr. Ione Wilson Simpson comes clicking into the kitchen.

"Hi, neighbors," she chirps. Ione is the Pentecost lady who lives next door with her husband Mitch and their son Butchie. The Pentecosts have a lot of rules—no drinking, no smoking. No haircuts, at least not on the women. Marcus wonders how Ione stands up under all those rules. He wonders how Ione stands up under all that hair. The dump cookie recipe came from Ione.

"I was just preparing tomorrow's lesson when I saw you gentlemen come in. Thought I'd check up on you. Nothing naughty going on, I hope."

Ione teaches at Mid North Bible College. She taught Christian Married Life until the state cracked down and made them offer what at least sounded like real courses. Now she's teaching The Christian Tradition in English Literature. For weeks its been Percy Byshe Shelley this and Percy Byshe Shelley that. As if this was the first she'd heard of him. Marcus had asked, "Where'd you get your Ph.D., Ione? Kmart?" He'd warned her she'd better slow up on that Romantic poetry before she and Mitchell started hanging around in Como Park and seeking arousals and desires of the earthly kind.

"Aren't you a caution," Ione had said.

Marcus always makes flirtatious, suggestive cracks around Ione. Ione thinks black men are supposed to do that around white women. She laughs and giggles, purses her lips. Marcus doesn't imagine there's too much action next door. Mitch is sort of a lump.

Ione gives Ali a pat on the head. Ali is wearing headphones, reading. His T-shirt says "Afro, Mondo, Skateboard, Death."

"I see you're making dump cookies," Ione squeals. "Give Ione a taste."

"They're for my mother. She loves Ione's dump cookies."

"How *is* sister Gabriel?" Ione asks, concerned. Ione starts dumping more stuff from the pantries into the dough.

Marcus's mother is fine, except for the fact she's not speaking to Marcus because of the big fight at last Sunday's dinner. Marcus and his mother and LaDonna fight every Sunday at dinner. Last week LaDonna was in prison, Marcus won the fight, and his mother stopped speaking to him. She calls up every twenty minutes, sighs loudly into the phone and hangs up.

Marcus hopes Ione's dump cookies will make her feel better. Ione is spooning the dough onto cookie sheets.

"I talked to LaDonna this morning," Ione says. "LaDonna tells me that Christ is by her side helping her through this ordeal."

Marcus knows that what LaDonna is really doing is setting up a pornographic tape distribution network for the girls in Shakopee.

"For a little pin money," LaDonna says. LaDonna is never long between schemes. She fully expects Marcus to smuggle tapes into the prison inside bowls of Jello salad. LaDonna hopes her association with Ione makes her respectable. She asks Ione to pray for her, presents Ione to Marcus's mother as the sort of upstanding friends she merits.

Verda Gabriel says LaDonna is a heathen, as is everyone LaDonna knows.

Ione places the first batch of cookies into the oven. She is rehearsing a lecture called "The Good Woman of the English Novel."

"You know," Ione says, "those Brontë heroines were often upstanding models of Christian love."

Marcus thinks Ione is crazy. Ione is wearing a long chocolate brown skirt with a slit up the back and also a pink knit top. She has a great figure.

"Ione, did anyone ever tell you you dress like a waitress at a Mexican cock fight?"

Ione cackles hysterically. "I've got these cookies started," she says. "Switch pans every twenty minutes and ya'll will be ready just in time for Mother Gabriel's dinner. Four P.M., right?"

Marcus's mother has had dinner at four o'clock every Sunday probably for forty years. Roast meat, baked potatoes, green beans, rolls. Last week she made a leg of lamb in honor of LaDonna's imprisonment.

"I best see to my own dinner," Ione says. She opens the headphones away from Ali's ears. "You haven't been over to play with my Butchie lately."

"Been busy," Ali says, snapping the phones back into place.

Butchie is nine. Ali says he is sadistic, bizarre and retarded. Says Butchie claims his G.I. Joes are "bad boys" and gives them swirly shampoos in the toilet. Ali says that all their little uniforms have blue rings around the collar.

"So, Ione, what fabulous meal are you making for the little man today?" Marcus asks.

"Lipton orange chicken," Ione says. "It's a whole fryer, two packages of onion soup mix, and a can of frozen orange juice concentrate."

Ione will write that down for Marcus and put it in the three-by-five card box on the counter. It is a yellow box with orange daisies on it and it says "Ione's recipes" in Kroy type.

Ione will probably also make a dump cake. That's a can of fruit cocktail dumped over a package of yellow cake mix. Much easier than dump cookies, but Marcus's mother won't eat fruit cocktail because maraschino cherries change the color of her stool.

"My best to your momma," Ione says.

"One more thing," Marcus stalls her. "Why is it you Pentecostal gals have such nice behinds?"

Ione giggles, says "Have a nice supper," and goes running out the back door.

"That whole family is retarded," Ali says, not bothering to either look up from the magazine or switch off the Walkman.

Ali announces that if supper with Grandma is to be anything like last week he'd as soon stay home and eat chicken with Ione. Ali often walks into Ione's dining room unannounced to sit down and eat. He wears his headphones so he won't have to listen to their chatter.

Marcus hands Ali the shaving cream, streamers, and balloons and orders him to get busy on the Bronco.

Marcus doesn't think last week's dinner was so bad. It was about a six on a scale of one to ten, with a one being the times that no one says anything, and a ten being the time LaDonna and his own mother had circled the dining room table with carving knives, each threatening to show the other how the big girls play.

Last week Marcus's mother met them at the door in a black dress, dabbing at her eyes with a white linen hanky.

"Somebody die, Ma?" Marcus asked.

All the shades were drawn in the house. Mrs. Gabriel waved her hand as if she couldn't speak.

Ali said, "What's up, Verda?"

She grabbed Ali and hugged him and kissed him and said that everything would be all right and not ever to call her by her given name again.

"What's her problem?" mouthed Ali.

"Are you feeling all right, Verda? I mean Mother."

Verda straightened her back, shook her head, and said dinner was getting cold.

At Sunday dinner Mrs. Gabriel sits at the head of the table in her late husband's place. With big puppy dog eyes she offered the lamb, the potatoes, the rolls.

"Now I'll say grace," she said. "Lord help us," she prayed, and then burst into tears. Ali mumbled "Jesus Christ" under his breath.

"What's wrong, Mother? Did they cancel 'The Wheel of Fortune'? Is Oprah on vacation?"

Mrs. Gabriel composed herself. She bravely picked at her lamb roast. Finally she could no longer hold back the stream of tears.

"A terrible thing has happened. Do you remember Mrs. Coles's son, Terrance?"

"Oh yeah, old Terry, went to the U."

Mrs. Gabriel sniffled a few times. "Well . . . he's joined the homosexuals." She said that and burst into a crying fit.

Ali fell off his chair, laughing. Marcus put down his fork, disgusted.

"Really, Mother," he'd said. "First of all: the homosexuals is not a club you join like the Elks."

Mrs. Gabriel cried louder.

"Furthermore: everybody knew that Terry gave twenty-five cent blow-jobs in the alley all through junior high school."

Marcus's mother turned off the tears instantly, stood at her place dry-eyed, ordered Ali to get up. "Go upstairs and get me an aspirin. Move it."

Ali got up; Marcus knew he would stand outside the door listening.

"This is a small community, Marcus. How is a black woman supposed to be able to hold her head high."

"I figured we'd get around to LaDonna," Marcus said.

"She's gone too far this time," Mrs. Gabriel said.

"Mother, you know full well LaDonna's been in jail before."

Mrs. Gabriel cringed. Marcus jumped to LaDonna's defense.

"She's gone straight, you know that. If the loan check had cleared the bank LaDonna would have owned the deed outright. She'd be ten thousand dollars richer today."

"A thieving little shrew," Verda seethed.

"It's called no-down-payment real estate. People do it all the time."

"And go to jail for it."

"You're blowing this out of proportion: she wrote a bad check."

"For five thousand dollars, Marcus. You're married to the biggest bunko artist west of Chicago."

"You know we're not married. And don't talk about LaDonna that way. She's gone straight. For good this time."

This Marcus feels is true. From prison LaDonna has announced plans for Madame LaDonna's Herbal Beauty Care.

"I won't have that woman in this family."

"She's not in your family: she's in mine."

Mother Gabriel clasped the sides of her head. "There it is again. Shame heaped on top of disgrace." She collapsed in her chair and let her head loll to the side.

Which is when Marcus broke the rules. Usually the big blow up came after desert, when Mrs. Gabriel would announce she'd heard enough and show them to the door. She and LaDonna would pass each other and go, "Humph." Last week Marcus had reached his limit. Was it not enough the miserable hours he spent deprived of the magical LaDonna, the long evenings, the lonely nights. But to have this, his own mother be so insensitive. Marcus called Ali in from his listening post.

"I won't give you the satisfaction of throwing me out of this dump. Let's go to McDonald's, son. Get a decent Sunday dinner for a change."

They strutted out that door and down the walk just like pimps. Marcus blew the horn all the way down Portland to the corner of Lexington Avenue.

Marcus takes the last batch of dump cookies from the oven. He has placed the already cool cookies into a Famolare shoebox for his mother. He will take the others to LaDonna out at Shakopee, maybe with a hot film, maybe not. LaDonna says to wear something sexy so she can show him off to the girls.

Ali comes in and stuffs a dump cookie in his mouth.

"Got that car ready?"

"Ready to roll," Ali snuffles. Ali has hung streamers and balloons from every place they could be tied. With shaving cream he has drawn an anarchy symbol on the hood, and written "Verda's Boys" on the side doors and windows.

"Sunglasses up and ready," Marcus orders. They give each other Elvis Presley sneers, burn rubber as they pull away from the curb. Marcus puts an old Santana cassette in the tape player. They cruise down Grand Avenue ten miles over the speed limit. Carlos's wild guitar screams from the windows.

"Wanna go to Mount Rushmore next week?" Marcus asks.

"Don't we have to visit LaDonna?"

"LaDonna's busy mixing Noxema with oregano. Ione will look after her."

"Let's do it," Ali says.

They stop the Bronco in front of Marcus's mother's large frame house. The house with the steep green lawn is stately, even elegant in the afternoon sun. Neighbors point, smile and wave at them.

Marcus takes the cookies and a bullhorn from behind the seat. They pose on the boulevard, hands on their hips.

"May I have your attention, please." Marcus says into the bullhorn. The words echo in the wide screen porch which covers the front of Verda Gabriel's house. "Attention, Verda. You are surrounded: open the door at once. Your boys are here and they've brought dump cookies."

There, the two of them stand, grinning in their big dark glasses. Behind his father's head Ali makes bunny ears with his fingers. They can see her in there, in the picture window, peeking out, checking for Mormons and homosexuals. Her hands first cover her mouth and then are on her hips in defiance.

They know where she's gone, stomping out of her formal parlor. She's clenching her fists, checking herself in the mirror, cursing at them under her breath. She's setting the table, checking the roast, smiling as she decides how, after a dessert of dump cookies a-la-mode, she will make those two heathens pay for this little stunt.

Steps to a New and More Wonderful You

Step One: Keep a positive outlook

In the Cool Whip container the mixture of Noxema and dried basil resembles lumpy potato chip dip. She mashes, she stirs, she whips. As hard as she tries she cannot get the dry gray-green flakes to dissolve.

What LaDonna needs is a mortar and pestle, but that is not the sort of thing they provide you with at the Shakopee Women's Detention Center.

She thinks she might ask one of the guards to help her, but doesn't expect that to get her anywhere. These women are so . . . functional. They walked around looking down on people just like high school gym teachers. They insisted on being called Miss Sherman and Mrs. Ekdahl and Ms. Supelveda. In return they called you by your given name. LaDonna has no time for such foolishness. She calls all the guards Shultzie, believes most of them are named that in real life and have made up names so they can detach themselves from working here. After calling a skinny, drab one Shultzie, she got hauled in front of the prison director, a square, pinch-faced woman, supposedly named Mrs. Indahar, whose clothes and skin were all the same washed out color of gray.

"You understand from your orientation we have rules here," this Indahar woman said. "For the protection of the staff, and for your protection as well."

LaDonna rolled her eyes. If she'd heard this speech once, she'd heard it a million times.

"You are expected to be out of your room and to your job on time."

Right, like she was going to spend all day in some smelly steamy laundry, washing a bunch of other women's underwear.

"You will be treated the same as the other women. If you are sick, report to the Dispensary. If you have a problem, report it to the guards."

"No problem," LaDonna had said.

"Also, you will address our staff in the way you were instructed. I hope that's clear. Despite your incarceration, you are encouraged to do your best. Our model girls earn extra privileges, you know. If there are no more questions . . ."

LaDonna had plenty of questions. First, why so many rules? Rules on when to get up, rules on when to go to bed, rules on whom you could talk to, rules on when you could talk to them. And where. For heaven's sake, they even had a line painted down the floor you had to walk on when you traveled the halls. They made you wear blue denim jumpers. In her real life LaDonna never wore blue, denim, nor anything remotely resembling a jumper. And you couldn't dress it up with a scarf or anything, and they took away all your jewelry at the gate. It was worse here than any of the jails she'd been in before. It was no wonder the girls here were so . . . tense and cranky. No wonder they looked depressed.

LaDonna knew their problem. These girls lacked dignity and self respect. They had never been allowed to achieve their full potential.

They had never unleashed the goddesses within themselves. That was why she was developing Madame LaDonna's Herbal Beauty Care Products. If only she had a mortar and pestle, she could test her first product—Madame's Neutralizing Facial Flush. She could test it on the girls in the recreation room.

There was one guard who might help her. The blond one with the big behind—she was a nice person, a regular person just like out in the real world. She wouldn't stand in the way of these girls becoming the best they could be.

LaDonna goes to the TV lounge to find her. There she is—pacing the back of the room, trying to look as if she isn't listening in on people's personal conversations, which is, after all, what she gets paid to do.

"Excuse me, Shultzie?"

The blond turns her back from the others. "LaDonna, please. My name is Mrs. Resnik. If you don't stop calling me Shultzie, I'm going to have to report you."

LaDonna sighs. "Whatever. Look: do you happen to know where they keep the mortar and pestle around here?"

Mrs. Resnik just looks at LaDonna with her mouth open. "The what?" she asks. She is a pretty pink-cheeked woman with yellow curls around her head like an angel. She isn't fat, but she has a big butt which isn't helped by the ill-fitting uniform all the officers wear. Charcoal gray, which LaDonna thinks is a disgusting color, fit only for the upholstery in bus depots.

"You know," LaDonna says. "A cup thing with a post thing with a knob on the end. For grinding aspirins and stuff. You *know* what I mean. Where do you keep it?"

"If you're sick . . ."

"Never mind. How about . . . do you have a mini food processor? Yay big." LaDonna indicates the size of a bowling ball.

"LaDonna, I don't know quite where you think you are, but this is a women's prison. You ask me for the most outrageous things. Baby oil, dried rose petals. Cucumbers. Do you have any idea what cucumbers go for in a place like this? You need to get real."

"You know, Shultzie, just because a person makes one little mistake doesn't mean her life comes to an end."

Just then a commotion breaks out by the TV. One of the prisoners has buried her head in her hands and is sobbing. The other girls have gathered around to comfort her. Shultzie rushes over to investigate. It is the new girl who is sobbing. The one in the room next to LaDonna. She is thin enough to see the outline of her bones and has wispy hair the color of rat's fur. LaDonna has noticed her. She is a girl who could use a lot of improvement.

STEP TWO: MAKE A FRESH START EACH DAY

LaDonna watches as the other girls gather up the weepy one and help her to her room. She steps out of the way—some of these girls are big and mean-looking. They keep razor blades in their cheeks, know karate, Kung Fu, and more ways to hurt you than a month's worth of Friday the 13th movies. They are the kind of girls who like to give orders. LaDonna knows better than to mess with them. Shultzie, who stands there doing nothing, would be of no help should LaDonna get into it with one of them. The girls are saying comforting things such as "Come on, honey," and "We understand." It doesn't do much good. The new girl weeps harder.

LaDonna knows what the poor creature needs. She needs a boost, needs to feel better about herself. She needs to realize the full potential of her womanhood. She needs Madame LaDonna's Neutralizing Facial Flush.

These girls wouldn't know that. Big, horsey, coarse gals. Shoplifters, pickpockets and whores. They were the sort of girls who hid your bra while you were in the shower in gym class. The whole herd steamrolls by, practically carrying the weepy one away. LaDonna presses close to the wall. It is unfair, she thinks. There should be separate prisons for girls like me. One prison for the criminals and one for the nice girls. Girls who have only made a little mistake.

And the truth of the matter: it was not she who made a little mistake. If only those banks had more integrity. Cash a check and they charge your account before you fold the bills and put them away, but try depositing a check, well, then it's three weeks before they get around to crediting your account. The president of the bank: he's the person who should be locked up. And that judge.

Really, it was a perfectly legitimate business deal. And, if you were to believe the people on cable television, absolutely foolproof, and there was no reason why LaDonna oughtn't be ten thousand dollars richer today rather than cooling her heals in some squalid women's prison.

LaDonna did everything just the way the man on the TV show, Kent Worthington, had said to do it. She found a house on Dayton Avenue that any fool could tell was going for cheap. She heard from her friend Cassie who heard from another friend who worked in the city planner's office that a cartel of Japanese businessmen was looking for real estate investment in St. Paul. The right buyer, the right seller, the right price. That was what Kent Worthington called the golden triangle. Kent said all you had to do was to activate the golden triangle, and money would pour into your pockets like water from a bottomless well. And all it was supposed to cost her, according to Kent, was the one dollar that the city wanted to get rid of the abandoned duplex, and a promise to pay the back taxes. Kent said that no-down-payment real estate was fool-proof, and LaDonna knows she is no fool. She had the Japanese businessmen sold on the property before they even saw it. She took them by on a sunny March afternoon, just after a snowfall. The snow covered the garbage, and the sun created flashes of bright light which blinded their eyes to the superficial flaws on the exterior of the building. She chose two P.M. so that the loud, filthy urchins of the neighborhood would be at school and not lower the value of her property with their presence.

"Gentlemen, here it is," LaDonna had said. They had given LaDonna their names, but LaDonna is not good with names. She called them "gentlemen" or "my little friends." She let them in through a side door which she had pried open with a crowbar earlier in the day. The man at the city assessors office told her she could have the key at closing time—details, details, details.

The place was a mess. There were holes in the walls, holes in the ceilings. The floors in many places were rotted clear through to the joists. LaDonna talks that to her advantage.

"Really, my little friends," she said. "Think of the possibilities. You can make this place into anything you want it to be. And, of course, I'll give it to you dirt cheap."

In the car the Japanese businessmen offered LaDonna fifteen thousand dollars. Despite her inclination to talk them up to twenty, she took it, savoring the fact that after the one dollar to the city, and the five thousand dollars in taxes she was nine thousand nine hundred and ninety nine dollars richer than she had been that morning. She asked for five thousand dollars—earnest money she called it, because that is what she had always heard it called before. She rushed to the bank with the check so that she could cover the check for five thousand which she'd written to the tax assessor earlier that same day in order to get the key, which he still wouldn't give her until the check cleared the bank.

In court LaDonna tells Judge McDonald pretty much the same story.

"So, technically speaking, your honor," she said, "having been the person who activated the golden triangle, I am entitled to whatever profits come from the transaction."

Over his glasses the judge gave LaDonna a look of disgust. How rude and unprofessional, she thought. For court she had worn her flowing crimson skirt, the one that is dotted with berries and bees. She had a wide black-fringed shawl wrapped around her waist.

At his disgusted look, she wheeled away from him dramatically and flounced to her seat. She grabbed her man Marcus's hand.

"I don't think that judge likes me very much," she said. "I think he may be prejudiced. We may have to call the human rights commission."

Marcus's sweaty hand petted hers. He shook his head. He had been nervous and apprehensive for days. He thought it a bad idea for LaDonna to act as her own attorney, and suggested that maybe she shouldn't come to court dressed as a gypsy girl. "A simple business suit would do," he told her, as she wound another length of gold chain around her neck. He was an old fuddy duddy. She ignored him. That's why she loved him—because he was a fuddy duddy and because he was easy to ignore. And also because he was the sexiest man on earth. And she would take bets on that.

"Just one minute, Miss," the judge said. "Step right back up to this bench."

LaDonna sighed and rolled her eyes. "What is it?" she said. She stood with her hands on her hips.

"Just a few words before I pass sentence. First: you are aware that it is illegal to write checks against funds which do not exist?"

There was some snickering in the courtroom. LaDonna knew it was her snooty significant-other-in-law, Verda. She'd make that old bitch pay for that snicker. If it was her last act on earth, she would.

"Ah, hah," she said, raising a finger in the judge's face. "But, is it illegal to write a check for money which you know will be or ought to be in your account."

The judge was not impressed. He made a note with his pen and removed his glasses. "One other thing," he said. "You are also aware, I assume, it is illegal to transfer title to property that you do not own?"

LaDonna pursed her lips. "But, once again, your honor, is it illegal to transfer title to property which you, in fact, intend to own? I rest my case." She said this and spun with a flourish to face the gallery and bowed. Her son Ali, parked back there next to that bitch stood and applauded her. LaDonna waved and started for her seat.

"Get back up here," the judge said.

Marcus put his head in his hands.

The judge looked at LaDonna and shook his head. "You are a piece of work," he said.

"I am shocked, your honor. I am involved in a monogamous, stable, sexually very fulfilling relationship. That's my man right over there. Cute, light-skinned fellow. Whatever it is you're implying . . ."

The judge raised his hand to stop her. He squeezed his eyes closed and pinched the bridge of his nose. "I have your record here. Let's review a few key items, shall we: operating a bawdy house. Running an unlicensed and illegal gambling scheme. Trafficking in stolen goods. Haven't you learned anything, young lady? You can't get something for nothing."

LaDonna crossed her arms. She turned her back on the judge. It was no use explaining: she'd tried before. These judges just didn't listen. Throw a rent party and they call it "running a bawdy house." What was a person supposed to do? Get thrown out on the street? And she had no way of knowing that those watches were stolen. As if all those big department stores got receipts from all their suppliers, too. And she'd even lost money on that Three Card Monte game. Stupid white folks in Rice Park . . . they always knew just where the damn queen was.

"Turn around and face me," the judge ordered.

"Honestly," LaDonna mumbled. She had no intention of turning around. America had gotten so bad. How was a business woman supposed to make a decent living anymore. Look at poor Mrs. Hillary Rodham Clinton. Try to make a few bucks for yourself and they nail you to a cross.

"Turn around," the judge shouted.

LaDonna faced him and gave him the evil eye.

Judge McDonald's jowls shook. "Despite the fact that no one lost money or property, it seems to me you show no remorse nor any real understanding of the possible harm that could come from such activity. I'm sentencing you to twenty days. Your time begins today."

LaDonna reared back into a horse stance, squinched her eyes, and pointed a finger at the judge. She dropped her voice to a guttural growl.

"May the stench of a thousand dead chickens afflict your every hour. May the dandruff from your eyelashes seal your eyeballs shut, blinding you forever."

"Five extra days. Contempt of court."

"May cats in heat circle your house every night for a year."

"Get her out of here."

The matron pulled LaDonna to the door. Through her fury she could see Marcus making slash marks at his throat, mouthing the words "enough already." In the back of the room, Verda dabbed at her crocodile tears, and, next to her, Ali stood, whistling and applauding, almost doubled-over with glee.

LaDonna interrupted her curses long enough to blow Marcus a kiss. "Call you from jail, honey," she shouted.

Marcus had his head in his hands. He looked afflicted. She knew that he hated her gypsy routines. He said they were kinda silly and undignified, said he wasn't sure that was how a black women ought to behave. He told her once that despite her full black hair and olive skin, in her babushka she looked more like Aunt Jemima than Maria Ospenskia. She had punched him in the stomach when he said that, and then felt so badly about it she treated him to a weekend in bed at the Crown Sterling Suites. Poor baby. There he was, exhausted, demoralized. The trial had been worse on him than it was on her. That was the problem with these sensitive, safe types. They were easily bruised, skittish. They didn't understand that you had to take chances to get anywhere in life, that you could be whatever you wanted to be if you just believed. They looked askance at big ideas, they distrusted schemes. LaDonna knew that secretly Marcus was as much invested in her plans as she was. Sometimes more so. It was the way he got his kicks. He was a vicarious sort of guy. She blew him one last kiss which he acknowledged with a feeble wave and with his shy sexy smile.

She pointed one last time at the judge. "May your wiener grow warts and fall off, you old crow."

Even the matron laughed at that.

Damn that judge, LaDonna thinks. Damn the bankers, damn the Japanese and damn Kent Worthington, too. LaDonna knows what her mistake has been. She's been too reliant on others. She hasn't used her own resources. She has been a fool, but no longer. Madame LaDonna's Herbal Beauty Care Products would see to that. She had a golden triangle all her own. The right woman with the right idea at the right time. She'd give American women what they wanted—high self-esteem and a clean complexion to boot. Stand back Avon. Watch out Elizabeth Arden. Mary Kay, you can eat my dust.

A shadow blocks the light from the hall, making the Noxema look ashy.

"Can I come in?" It is the mousey weepy girl from next door.

"Sure," LaDonna says. She offers the girl the chair by the window. The room is narrower than a car is wide. LaDonna has to roll back on the bed to let her by. The girl perches on the edge of the chair demurely. It is as if she has been called in for an interview with the warden—her back and her legs are held straight and stiff, and her hands are on her knees.

LaDonna dribbles some baby oil in a bowl. She watches the girl out of the corner of her eye. The girl stares at her hands or at the floor. Flanks of hair hang parallel to her head like blinders.

"Smells nice in here," the girl says. She has a small voice and a small smile.

"Does it really?" LaDonna bubbles. She has no idea. She has lived with the herbs and creams for so long she is immune. "Thanks," she adds. "What does it smell like? You know the smell is really important."

"I don't know. I couldn't describe it."

"Oh, come on. What would you say? Is it like a floral bouquet? Like lemon mist? Like an English herbal garden?"

"I'm not very good at this. I guess . . . maybe . . . maybe the latter. I guess."

"English herbal garden. Exactly what I thought. Don't sell yourself short, girl. You're very good at this. Now try this one." LaDonna removes the top of a round Rubbermaid container. "What do you think?"

"That's the Lemon Mist?" the girl asks.

"Well, actually it's just lemon juice now, but it will be Lemon Mist when I'm done with it."

"What exactly are you making in here?"

"I'm not quite prepared to say as of yet. And don't blab about the lemon juice. It's like an illegal substance around here. That, and the cucumbers. What's the story on that? Are they afraid a person might make a salad or something?"

The girl smiles, and that makes LaDonna relax. The gloom this girl carries surrounds her like a cloud of gnats.

"You always seem so busy," the girl says. "Carrying around bowls and jars and all kinds of things."

"Oh, yes, girl. LaDonna is always busy. Have to be. My mama says even as a baby I had something going in that crib all the time. Life's too short. Got to keep moving."

"So you're LaDonna. My name is Nancy."

"Nancy? Like Nancy Drew? I loved Nancy Drew. I read all those books. I have the whole set. I saved them. Was gonna give them to my little girl. But, then I didn't have any little girl, I had a little boy, Ali. That's his picture over there. He's twelve. Handsome, just like his father, of course. I love him. But what am I gonna do with those Nancy Drews? Ali, all he ever reads is skateboard magazines and comic books. He's a funny kid. Really. You should call him up. He'd have you cheered up in no time—bustin a gut. And it's not like I'm gonna have another baby on the chance it should be a girl just so I can pass some books along. It was so horrible that first time. I'm sure you know what I'm saying. Do you have any kids?"

Nancy nods. She looks at her feet.

"One kid? Two kids?"

"Two. A little boy and a little girl."

"Well, imagine that. A little thing like you. You left them with their daddy, I bet. Don't you worry one bit."

Nancy shakes her head.

"My Marcus—he's my man, that's his picture right there, that's what I call him—my man—we're not married or anything. He's just my man—he's a natural born daddy. Other people pay him to take care of their kids. He's a teacher, you know. Is something wrong, honey?"

"It's not fair," Nancy sobs. "I shouldn't be here."

"We have something in common then."

"I'll stay here forever. I don't care. He'll never get my kids. I'll never tell where they are. Damn that judge."

LaDonna rises. Though she isn't sure why, she feels vindicated and triumphant. "Yes, damn him," she says. "Damn that judge. Damn them all, all the judges everywhere."

STEP THREE: MAKE THE MOST OF WHAT YOU'VE GOT

LaDonna dumps another giant-sized clothes basket into the industrial drier. She heaves it up with a loud grunt, lets the basket crash to the ground, lets go a loud whiny sigh. Such torture. She drops to the floor by the machine. It is all she can do to press the button which starts the clothes tumbling. Some of the other women in the laundry give her dirty looks, but she doesn't care. It is hot in here and the machine is filled with sweat-stained jumpers and fat women's panties without any elastic. Just touching them makes her feel faint. LaDonna does not do laundry, not even at home. The Pentecost lady next door—Dr. Ione Wilson Simpson—does it for her. LaDonna never asks her to do it. She just barges in at nine-thirty every Wednesday morning like clockwork, sets on the table her stack of papers from the Mid-North Bible College to be graded, and puts in a load of wash. She has done this for six years since she and her husband Mitch and their son Butchie bought the house next door to Marcus and LaDonna in the Tangletown neighborhood of St. Paul. She takes LaDonna to the Rainbow Foods and makes her buy products such as Spray 'n Wash and fabric softeners. She seems to know what to do with such products—when to spray what on, and during which cycle. It is like some magical technological rite as far as LaDonna is concerned, and she tells Ione she just doesn't get it. Patient loving Christian woman that she is, Ione tells LaDonna that there are no secrets. It is all spelled out for you on the labels of clothes, on the boxes of detergent and inside the lid of the washer. LaDonna resists. She suspects a trap in there somewhere. While the clothes wash, she fills out sweepstakes letters and completes contest applications. Ione fluffs and folds, corrects papers for her course on the Christian Tradition in English Literature. They work right through *The Price is Right* and the first half of *The Young and the Restless*. Ione impresses LaDonna with her efficiency. While it might take LaDonna all morning to do her Publisher's Clearing House Sweepstakes entry, in that time Ione does two loads of laundry, copies all the new recipes out of *First* magazine onto three-by-five cards which she keeps in a box on the counter for Marcus's use, and grades thirty-five essays on the topic "What Jesus would say to Charles Dickens." And she is a whiz at *The Price Is Right's* Hi/Lo game. She always knows the exact price of the Dustbuster and the Wurlitzer organ with the burled cherry finish. LaDonna tells Ione that she should fly to California and be a contestant on the Price is Right, but Ione says that a Christian woman does not display herself in such a fashion. They both think, despite his animal rights convictions, Bob Barker should go back to brown hair. He was much cuter before.

The dryer vibrates through LaDonna's backbone. She cannot believe this is happening to her. The big gray-haired woman who runs the prison laundry comes over. She wears a white tunic and slacks and has a gray moustache. Her name badge says Shultzie—which just confirms LaDonna's theory.

"Let's go, Miss. This ain't a resort, you know."

"Isn't it time for a break yet?"

"You been working for twenty minutes. Let's go. I got a basket of hot sheets over here got your name on them. Up and at 'em, sister." She offers LaDonna a hand and LaDonna takes it. She aims LaDonna toward a rolling laundry cart of white sheets still steaming from the dryer.

"Let's get 'em folded before they wrinkle."

LaDonna sighs.

"These sheets wrinkle, girl, and you'll be down here ironing till the second coming. Get on the other end." Shultzie dangles a cigarette from the corner of her mouth and tosses LaDonna the other end of the sheet.

"What you in for, honey?" the cigarette dances at the corner of her mouth.

"There was some confusion about the balance in my checking account."

Shultzie shakes her head. "Yeah, that'll happen I hear. You got a man?"

Oh, yeah. I got me a man, LaDonna thinks. Quite a man indeed. She misses Marcus so, it has turned into a pain—a pain she feels in her chest. It burns as if she has swallowed a glowing charcoal briquette.

"Yes, there is a man," she answers.

"Don't let that sheet drag, girl. We're not doing this laundry over on account of you."

LaDonna raises her end of the sheet as high as her shoulders. It might be light as down, but weighs on her arms like lead. It is she who must walk her end of the linen over to match Shultzie's—Shultzie won't budge. When the sheet is folded small enough, Shultzie slaps it on the table as if it were a steak, and then irons it with the flat of her hand.

"So, this man," she asks LaDonna. "What was it he done to you got you in here?" She snaps another length of hot cloth in LaDonna's direction.

LaDonna flinches, but catches the sheet before it hits the cement floor.

"Nothing. He didn't do a thing."

Shultzie stops to stub out the cigarette. "Come on, girlie. There's a man in there somewhere. Gotta be. What he do? Steal your kid's milk money? Hide some crack in your purse? Pretty gal like you: Bet he had you out on the street."

LaDonna is incensed at the woman's regressive attitude. It is the 1990s: Where was this woman's head? Had it never occurred to her a woman might be able to get into prison without the help of a man?

"You got it all wrong Shultzie. My man's completely innocent."

"Girlie, there aren't any of them innocent, not a one. You in here doing time for some man's crime. He's out there got his peter stuck up every piece of snatch he can find."

"Never," screams LaDonna. She balls up her end of the sheet and throws it in Shultzie's face. Never ever. Not her Marcus. He wouldn't. He loved her and she him. And, furthermore: she owned him. Not just his heart and soul, but him, all of him. She bought him. Outright. Paid good cash money at a charity auction at the University of Minnesota.

She hadn't gone there to shop, really. It was back during her student radical days, and she and the sisters from Imani—the African Women's consciousness-raising group—had gone to the annual fraternity row "slave auction" to protest the trivialization of the greatest tragedy in American history, as well as the general racism of the campus Greek system. LaDonna, in a floor-length red, black and green skirt, carried a sign reading "Save Our History." She had hand-lettered it herself between her art history and her marketing classes. Her plan—all the sisters' plans—was to turn that farce out. Get up on that stage and show their behinds if necessary. The field house was dressed for spring carnival in balloons and crepe paper, the stage framed with fake columns and pilasters. Center stage one of those Nordic frat types posed in front of a platform for display of the merchandise. He was dressed as a southern gentleman, riding crop and all.

LaDonna remembers rage souring her stomach. She wanted to kill every damn honky in that room.

Just as she and the Imani sisters made ready to charge the stage, they brought him out.

"Fine looking specimen we got here now," the slave master drawled, his round Minnesota accent sifting through a poor imitation of Southern speech. Marcus, stripped to the waist, had one of those cheap hippy tapestries wrapped around him. "Haven't had a buck like this one on display for many years," the auctioneer continued. Marcus primped and flexed his muscles. He strutted around the block. The next day he told LaDonna he was so stoned he didn't know where he was. Up under the field house lights his oiled brown body had sparkled like patent leather.

LaDonna remembers biting her hand.

"What am I bid for this brown beauty?"

"This is an outrage," yelled sister Aisha.

"You should be ashamed," yelled sister Folani.

"Fifty dollars," yelled LaDonna.

"Sister Yaguama," the others scolded. LaDonna was going by her African name full-time back then. Yaguama El Hakim. These days she only used that name when she wanted to intimidate Ali's teachers or the people at traffic court.

"I have fifty dollars from the young lady right back here. Can I get fifty-five dollars?"

LaDonna bought Marcus for seventy dollars. She could have had him for fifty had it not been for sister Yasmin, who bid Marcus up through the fifties and sixties at two dollar increments. And despite the judgmental look on her face, LaDonna knew Yasmin really wanted him. Wanted him bad, too. Why did black women have to be so damn competitive? If she wanted one she should have waited until the next one came up, but no, she had to bid against a sister, take hard earned dollars out of LaDonna's pocket. LaDonna put Marcus on her Mastercard and said good-bye to Imani forever.

"Get your ass off that dryer and get over here and pick up this sheet," Shultzie orders.

LaDonna sits on top of a large machine, her back to the room. There is no place to hide in prison. All the rooms are locked and everywhere there are guards. The dryer is oversized—all out of proportion like doll house furniture. She knows she looks foolish up here, but she won't let them see her cry, not ever. Not these coarse heifers. How many of them had what she had? How many of them had nice houses in good neighborhoods? How many of them owned their own businesses? How many of them owned their own man?

"There'll be trouble for you, girl, and I mean it. Get down now."

Not her man. Not Marcus. Not ever.

As punishment LaDonna must sit through the prison's evening group therapy sessions. They meet next to the TV lounge in a cinder block room which is decorated to look like a poor person's living room. The sofa and chairs have been upholstered in brown and green stripes. They look soft, but are hard as if they were made of bricks. On one wall a bad seascape has a ketchup stain—or is that the sun—and there is an enormous orange wall hanging opposite it. LaDonna has no idea what it is supposed to represent.

A man who looks like Jimbob Walton runs the group therapy sessions. He places the furniture in a circle and encourages the women to bring their coffee and knitting. The group meets every night at seven-thirty, and about ten women show up. A few like LaDonna and Nancy have been ordered to do so, but some, LaDonna knows, come to lust over Dr. Jimbob. She hears how they carry on about him in the dining room. They speculate on how big he is and how long he might last. LaDonna doesn't know what the attraction is—but then skinny redheads never did do anything for her. And, of course, she had Marcus at home. She couldn't wait to show him off to these crones. That would really give them something to talk about.

"Shall we begin, ladies?" LaDonna sits with Nancy on a love seat. There are knitters and rug hookers and tappers and twiddlers. She and Nancy are the only ones with idle hands.

"I thought tonight we would just have a general bull session. Let's get out what's bothering us. Who wants to begin."

LaDonna rolls her eyes. This is her third meeting. They never got anywhere here. It was one hard luck story after another. How this one got caught up in drugs and how that one wished she'd paid more attention in school. And, of course, everyone's man done them wrong. No wonder that old witch in the laundry was so cynical. Twenty years of listening to this shit.

Tonight there are no takers. The women rock and twiddle and knit in silence.

"Anyone?" Dr. Jimbob prompts.

"We ain't heard from them two." A hard-looking blond indicates LaDonna and Nancy.

"Strictly volunteer here," Dr. Jimbob says. "No coercion in the group."

"Just trying to make 'em feel welcome," the blond says. She gives LaDonna and Nancy a gap-toothed smile. Her hair has been treated with chemicals until it is just lifeless straw on her head. "It's really helped me to open up, these sessions. I feel like I'm getting my shit together. Dr. Lallaburton here is a great listener."

LaDonna had been there the night the blond "opened up." She had told a lurid story which involved being the only female companion of a

Puerto Rican motorcycle gang from Chicago. She apparently still loved the leader, a Manuelito, who, according to blondie, was "an all right dude if he would just cut out some of the funky shit he was into." LaDonna has been horrified by all these women's stories. She realizes that, despite the fact she does not do laundry, cook, nor do housework of any kind, compared to most of these women she is the ideal middle American housewife. And, in addition to her general disdain for such public confessionals, LaDonna finds herself shamed into silence. She is ashamed to admit how relatively ordinary and decent her life is. Their lust after her story sickens her. They want to know all about her—what horrible things she's done and who she's done them with. She is tempted to make up a tale, make herself a Mafia gun moll, voodoo priestess, queen of the gypsies. They would have no way of knowing what was true. She could be whatever she wanted. She had always heard about honor among thieves, but she had never imagined it included competition to see whose life was the most immoral.

She is saved by Nancy. "I guess it's just that . . ." she begins, "you can talk about it and talk about it and it doesn't do any good. It doesn't change anything." She trembles and tears roll down her cheeks. LaDonna pats her arm.

"Nancy is right," LaDonna says. "All this dredging up the past is no good. How do you expect to get anywhere?"

The older black woman who has been knitting speaks up. "Well, baby, sometimes it just helps to have someone listen to you. Dr. Lallaburton says we can't deal with our own troubles until we face them. Talking about them is the first step."

LaDonna isn't sure how to react to the woman. Her name is Mattie. She means well, reminds LaDonna of her mother, and in fact they have committed the exact same crime, except Mattie, unlike LaDonna, was actually buying things with her checks. But unlike LaDonna, she had no intention of rushing to the bank with a perfectly good check drawn on the Bank of Tokyo which ought to have more than adequately covered her expenses.

And all of these women—so impressed with Dr. Jimbob. What did he do but sit there with his mouth open and nod his head? Sure, you can sit there and make notes on your little pad, but can you make Swiss steak with mashed potatoes and creamed peas? Her Marcus could, and he scrubbed a toilet like nobody's business, was great in bed, and meanwhile, here sat this fraud pretending to help people with their problems.

"So," LaDonna says. "We talk and we talk and we talk. And then, what? What happens next? You wave some magic wand and the problem goes away? That's bullshit and every one of you knows it. You want to fix a problem, you make a plan. You figure out what you need to do, you go out and do it."

The women look from LaDonna to Dr. Jimbob, waiting for him to do something. To scold her or encourage her or pat her on the back or slap her on the face. He smiles and nods.

"There's not a plan anywhere to help me," Nancy sobs.

"You mustn't say that," LaDonna says, grabbing both of Nancy's hands. "Never say that. There's always hope. It's like driving—what they tell you in driver's ed: Always look for an out. Sometimes it's hard to see, but it's there. You make your plan and you stick with it. If it doesn't work, you go on to your next plan. And the next one and the next one. Until you get where you need to be."

Nancy sniffled. "You really believe that will work for me?" She looks at LaDonna and her eyes fill with hope.

"Your friend is very wise," Dr. Jimbob says.

Yes, wise, LaDonna thinks. I am wise. And, the flash in her brain is what she thinks they must be talking about when they show light bulbs going off above your head in cartoons. Madame LaDonna's Herbal Beauty Care Products are not enough. There must be a book. A book to tell these woman how to release their inner beauty, just as the creams and lotions enhance the surface. A step by step plan. The man says she is wise, and the man is a doctor.

There must be a book.

STEP FOUR: PAY ATTENTION TO THE DETAILS

LaDonna has found that if she peels cucumbers and removes the seeds, then whips them up with baby oil and egg whites, she has a cream as light as sea foam. Rose petals turn the mixture a pale pink and makes it smell sweet and irresistible. Unfortunately, leave it on the counter overnight and it turns black. Refrigeration should solve that, and surely

American women are willing to give up a little space in the ice box for a chance at a whole new life.

Nancy comes in and plops on the bed. The swelling around her eyes has decreased—she must be crying less—but she has taken to biting her thumbnail. Perhaps she has run out of tears.

"I've been thinking about what you said. At the session the other night."

"I was just talking," LaDonna says. "Those people get me so upset."

"No. It was great. I needed to hear that. I want to believe you, too. I do, really, but I just don't know."

LaDonna sits facing Nancy on the edge of the bed. She feels a pounding in her chest. She had been heard and listened to. She has the power, the gift. She knows she can do this.

"I believe there is a way out of almost anything," she says. "Sometimes it doesn't seem that way—I know that I've been in some tough jams. But I never give up."

Nancy takes her thumb from her mouth, folds her hands on her lap. "My husband is a powerful man," she says. "I was attracted to him because he was powerful. He had money and charm, as well. I fell into his trap. Let myself be led around by the nose. He was good to me. He gave me whatever I wanted. You can lose your soul with such a person. I guess that's what I did. I lost my soul because I wanted what he offered. I thought it was such a good life. I never expected to want for anything.

"We had our kids and they were perfect. My boy and my girl. Life was sweet. I imagine I could have continued like that for another fifteen or twenty years. I kept busy. Looking after him and the kids. And I joined committees and served on boards. All of that activity and money is like a drug. It has a way of numbing your mind. It obscures what is really going on around you.

"When my daughter told me that her daddy had hurt her, I didn't really understand what she was saying. She was only six and she didn't have the words to talk about it. And the person she was telling me about was my husband, after all. A man I thought I knew. I wasn't equipped to hear what she was telling me. Who would be?

"The pediatrician was quite good at her job. She didn't pull any punches. She talked about penetration, ruptures, abrasion. All those sorts of things. She tried to warn me what I was about to go through.

"From that moment I operated on instinct. Do you believe in instinct, LaDonna? I sent the children to my mother in Illinois. The bastard denied everything. Of course. First he said it must have been someone else. Then—on his attorney's advice—he claims that his own daughter is a liar. That nothing of the kind has ever happened. That the doctors are frauds. I was given an ultimatum. Go along with his defense or get out. Call my own daughter a liar in court in front of all those people, or get out. Great choice, huh?

"I left and he came after me with everything his money and power could muster. Restraining orders, subpoenas, divorce papers. He closed all the joint bank accounts, canceled all my credit cards. I hardly had bus fare, let alone money to hire a lawyer.

"I don't know how he did it. With money you can do anything. He made a liar out of her. Despite the evidence. Made his own daughter—a six-year-old child—into a liar, right there in court. They ordered her returned home. To his home. But that will never happen. Not as long as I'm alive. There's a network of us out there. Mothers who are sick of the bullshit from the social workers and the judges and the lawyers and the courts. They are supposed to be looking out for the children, and they send them back to something like that? Not as long as I'm alive. I've sent my children away to keep them safe. To be honest I don't even know where they are. I know they are safe and with people who care for them. I know how to find them when I need to. The judge says I'm to stay here until I produce my children." Nancy shakes her head.

"I believe you, LaDonna. I mean, I have to believe you that there is a way out of this. A way I can keep my children safe. I can't go on feeling hopeless. I'm ready to make a plan. Will you help me, LaDonna?"

In the jar LaDonna has mixed lemon juice, Ivory liquid, and yogurt. She stirs with a long wooden spoon. The mixture has the consistency of glue. She knows she must make it thicker.

"I just need a sensible voice. Someone to shake me up. Someone like you, LaDonna. You can help me."

She thinks about her man, Marcus. A man she thinks of as belonging to her. A man who has often to her been like a joke—a joke that she could tell people and they would laugh and she would feel good because the joke was a joke that she made, and because the joke made it like it wasn't real and she did not have to take him seriously. Did not have to imagine that he might be another kind of man other than the kind of man he was. A man like the man this woman chose. Her Marcus. Her man. A man who had only ever confirmed what she knew the first time she saw him, there, shining, under the lights in the field house. That she would melt into the story of his life like butter into warm bread.

Nancy hops off the bed and starts pacing the narrow room. "I'm getting my kids back," she says, and LaDonna feels blessed. She has a man and she has a son and they are good to each other and they are good to her. They bring her herbs and gels and inedible cookies they have made with their own hands. They listen to her stories and her plans and her schemes. They tell her it will all come true just as she says. They tell her she is beautiful. They sit with her on the ugly plaid couch in the cinder block room and hold hands.

"You're gonna help me, aren't you LaDonna."

LaDonna keeps thinking about Marcus and Ali. It is something she knows how to do.

"Yes," she says. "I'll help you. Yes."

STEP FIVE: NEVER GIVE UP HOPE

LaDonna writes the final formula for Madame's Neutralizing Facial Flush in her journal. It is a secret. On one page she has sketched possible designs for the label. On another page she has begun outlining her book: *Ten Steps to a New and More Wonderful You*. Each chapter will be one of the ten steps, but so far she has only been able to think of five of them.

Nancy appears in the door. She is laughing and tears are dripping off her chin.

"Not again," LaDonna says.

"I'm a mess," Nancy laughs.

"Come on in. I'm all ready for you."

"You've thought of something. You have a plan."

"Come over here," LaDonna says. Using a spatula she smears Madame's Neutralizing Facial Flush around Nancy's face. She smears extra on the cheeks where the tears keep washing it away.

"How does it feel?" LaDonna asks.

"It's cold," Nancy says. "So cold."

"We leave it on for just a second. It's only the first step. Go ahead and rinse."

Nancy pats her face with a towel, just the way LaDonna instructs. "What if it doesn't work?" she asks.

"Look," LaDonna says. She frames Nancy in the mirror and stands behind her. She outlines Nancy's jaw with her hands. "Look. Can't you see? You're positively glowing."

"Yes," Nancy says. Her eyes are shining and alive. "Yes. I see. I see."

Busted: A Boy's True Tale of Real Life in a Big City Junior High School

I hate my life. I hate school, I hate all teachers, I hate St. Paul. Some days I hate my mom and dad and Verda. I especially hate Mr. Smutts and Ione's little boy Butchie, who is a sick mental.

There is probably a big sign over my head that says, "It's all his fault." It has a big red arrow pointing in my direction at all times.

Here is an example. I am walking down the hall of Hennepin Junior High School. It is hell on earth here and that is not an exaggeration. The toilets are always overflowing, the food is rancid, and Troy Jackson told me that he saw a rat in the boys' locker room carrying off someone's tennis shoe, and I believe him because he is one of the few people here who is not a dweeb. It was in the middle of second period and I had just gotten to school because Marcus, who is my dad, did not get out of bed in the morning to go to his own job until almost nine because he says he is tired, but really he is depressed because LaDonna, who is my mom, is in jail. So I was late too, though it was not my fault as you can see. Mr. Smutts, who is the assistant principal and who is known to be real mean and hateful, stops me in the hall.

"What's your name, young fella?"

I do not like being called things like young fella. Please, remember that. Thank you.

I put up my hands. I figure there is less chance they will shoot you if you just throw up your hands. Mr. Smutts is wearing a suit which has more colors in it than they have flavors at Baskin Robbins. He is a white man who is one of those white men who is all the same color. He is the color of Cheerios. He is probably wearing that suit so he does not fade into the walls. In response to what is my name I say, "Huh?"

"You come with me," he says.

So, I am under arrest. Do not let anyone tell you you have Constitutional rights if you are twelve, because it is not true. You might as well live in Russia or one of those kinds of places.

I keep my hands up in the air and he puts his hand on my shoulder to walk me to the office. I know the way.

Please, do not ever touch me, thank you, not unless there is something crawling on me like a black widow spider, and especially not if you are the white principal of the junior high.

He takes me in a room that has chairs all around a table. There is going to be a meeting or something here, you just know it.

"Sir," I say, in my most weak and serious type voice. I can use this voice on my grandma Verda and she will give me cash or anything else. "Sir, can I ask you a question?"

"Put your hands down first," he says.

I drop my hands which slam down on the table because they have gone to sleep on me. Sometimes I lay on my back on my bed at home and just hold my arm up over my head and see how long I can keep it there. It hangs there almost like it was hanging from a string until it feels dead and like it isn't even attached to me anymore. Then it comes slamming down hard like it did just now and the blood comes rushing back in, all tingly and stuff. "Excuse me for living," I say.

"There's no excuse for your ilk," Smutts says, which is pretty much uncalled for, wouldn't you say, and ought to be reported to someone but a person wouldn't even know where to begin since, as we all know, they are all in it together.

"Forget it," I say, and he tells me to sit over there with the rest of them. The rest of them are Demetrius, LT, Tony J. and Cool. They are sitting in four chairs in front of a chalkboard. They are probably the four toughest people at Hennepin. You would not want to mess with them, even if you were the assistant principal. Marcus, who is my dad and who is also a teacher, says that when LT was in sixth grade he kicked out the ceiling tiles in the bathroom, touched a live wire and shorted out the electricity in a ten block area of St. Paul. Marcus said that LT said it only stung a little bit. Needless to say these are not the people I hang with. They all got on their shades and are dangling toothpicks from their mouths and snapping their gum. They are all leaned back with their feet up, casual. They could be at home watching *Yo! MTV Raps.* They all have on Raiders caps and lots of black clothes. It means they are in a gang or something even if this is only St. Paul and they would have you believe there are no problems here of any kind if you watch the news on TV. Just look around this room. Me, I am wearing a Vision Wear shirt and a really loud pair of jams. I stick out like dog doo in a snow bank.

Smutts slams down his fist. "Get those feet down. Get those glasses off. Sit up in those chairs. Now." Me, who was already down, off and up, have to put my hands on my knees to keep them from shaking. Next to me I notice the Wild Bunch seem to be shaking just a little bit too.

"You youngsters are in some serious trouble here, and I mean serious. We're talking police. I suggest your attitudes reflect it." Cheerios man has his hands clasped behind his back and is walking back and forth like a duck, his head bobbing up and down with each step. He's one of those popeyed dudes too. I'm trying to remember who it is he reminds me of.

"On this piece of paper you are to put down the full names and phone numbers of whatever adults claim to be responsible for you. Do it now. I suggest no foolishness."

Well, I guessed I was in quite a spot then, because, unlike my brothers in crime, whose mothers were probably at this minute at home watching the soaps, that is unless they were down at the bank cashing the welfare checks or standing doorwatch at some crack house, my life had recently gotten more complicated. First we have Marcus, who is supposed to be a teacher over at the Hawthorne School, which is apparently according to him and others, as much of a hell as this hellhole and is also full of a lot of crazy retards like Butchie Simpson the mental pervert who lives next door to me and whose mother has the biggest set of headlights I have ever seen. I know all about Hawthorne school because I actually went there for a month last year and it was so awful that I threatened to become bulemic if Marcus and LaDonna didn't get me out of there, and I actually had to drink four glasses of salt water and throw up on the Domino's Pizza to get them to believe me. Which was okay because we were all getting sick of Domino's anyway seeing as we have to have it twice or three times a week because Marcus gets too stressed out to cook and LaDonna claims to not understand really how the oven works even though Ione has given her lessons on a regular basis for as long as I can remember. Ione is a good cook, too, if you can stand the fact that she has to say a twenty-five minute prayer before each meal and then has to ask her husband Mitch how his day was. Mitch is a park ranger in Como, and he has to tell down to the last detail how his day was, including the exact number of squirrels he saw and how many didn't have tails. And Butchie who is only a couple of years younger than me and still plays with G.I. Joe, chews up his food and opens his mouth for me to see it and makes all kinds of perverted faces at me that make my skin crawl. I would not put up with this at all, but Ione is about the best cook there is. Even her meat loaf is good. I just eat right through the prayer and stuff. There's plenty. Who knows what Marcus and LaDonna eat. Sometimes school is so bad it is all Marcus can do to lay there on the couch and have LaDonna rub his feet. They lie there and eat bon-bons. They act like rich people except they don't have enough money. If Smutts calls Marcus and tells him I'm in trouble he will just have his usual anxiety attack and then he will do something like have the secretary go watch his class while he lays down for a few hours. And then there is LaDonna, who is a real estate agent, so she says, but she cannot be called because she is what Grandma Verda refers to as "temporarily incarcerated," which just means her butt is in jail for either attempted fraud or for putting a hex on the judge. I was there in court and I couldn't figure it out. All I know it was a pretty good show. And even if I did know the number of the Shakopee Women's Detention Center, I would not be giving it to Smutts. Right now *The Young and the Restless* is about to start. LaDonna has a special dispensation from the prison head doctor who says she is not to be disturbed during her favorite story because doing so would cause "undue psychological stress." She told me on the phone, LaDonna did. She also says the joint is chock full of chumps and anyone who couldn't work the angles out there was a pathetic wimp and a loser. And not that you'd want to let these people know that your mother is in jail anyway, especially since they would not understand, nor probably be very interested in the fact that she is basically a good person who has always had trouble balancing her checkbook and can be a little over-dramatic at times.

Which leaves Marcus's mother, Grandma Verda, who would have what Marcus calls a "conniption fit" if she got the call. She will blame the whole thing on the fact that I am a "poor unfortunate child with immature, irresponsible parents." She will have me down in custody court as fast as her fully-equipped Cadillac Coup deVille with cordovan leather seats, automatic windows and fully animated computerized dashboard can get us there. I will end up court-ordered to live in her house, which I like to refer to as "plastic slip cover city." It's a big white house over on Portland Avenue. Grandma puts coasters under the porcelain dogs. She is a little crazy. Besides, I can't remember the code for Tuesdays. It is either ring two times, hang up, ring two times, hang up, then call, or ring once, hang up, ring twice, hang up, then call. Otherwise Verda doesn't answer. It could be Mormons calling.

Just when the paper gets to me, I remember it is Ione's day off. Ione, whose whole name is Ione Wilson Simpson, is also a Pentecost lady, and she teaches at the Mid North Bible College out in the sticks somewhere, but because today is Tuesday and she only teaches on Monday,

Wednesday and Friday she will be home, and just like LaDonna, sitting in front of *The Young and the Restless,* except Ione will have her big behind perched on an exercise bike so she can continue to get compliments from Marcus who is always saying crude things to Ione like telling her she ought to put curb feelers on her hips and how her big hooters are enough to make any man want to go out and fight for his country. Either he is trying to make her blush or he really does think she has a "nice ass" which is what he is always telling her. Good old Ione. She parades around with all this hair on her head and a pair of cat eye glasses on a beaded chain. She'll come get me. I write her name down and her number and put the word guardian in parentheses. Cheerios takes it without looking and gives it to a woman out in the hall.

"Gentleman," he says. "A case of sexual misconduct has been reported to me this morning."

"Oh, man," some of the boys down the way mumble.

"I have reason to believe one or more of you is involved."

Oh, great, and what is this? Line up the usual suspects. Me? Ali Phillip Hank Aaron Gabriel (yes, those really are all my names for reasons which ought to be apparent). I am a person who has helped old ladies across the street without even having a scout uniform. (What a pack of wusses those guys are.) Yes, I do own and use my skateboard, but I always yield to pedestrians and never ride in front of cars. How did I get in the police line-up? Is snoring in class a crime? Is having a fashionable haircut? I look down the row: here I am like a goldfish in a barrel full of sharks.

"At the time of the incident you young men were found in the hallway, without passes. If any of you would like to step forward and own up to your behavior, you would be showing a lot of maturity and saving the rest of us a lot of grief." Smutts gives us all a look he thinks will melt stone. He thinks his beady eyes will squeeze a confession out of this crowd, but I know for a fact several of us here have lied our way out of tougher spots than this. I raise my hand.

"Uh, sir."

Smutts leans up with interest. He gets ready to take notes.

"What exactly is sexual misconduct?" I mean for all I know one of these guys is as perverted as Butchie, who punishes his G.I. Joes when they are bad by washing their nonanatomically-correct private parts with Brillo pads.

Smutts leans back and puts his hands behind his oat-colored hair. He purses his lips. "Fair enough," he says. "One of our female students claims she was touched inappropriately by a black male student. She said it happened in the hallway."

The brothers down the way exhale, shake their heads, sigh. "That's dog," Cool says.

I start to raise my hand and say, "Uh, sir," and I figure I'm gonna ask him what exactly touched inappropriately means. Was she like patted on the head? Did someone pick her nose and dig in her ears? I decide not to because I figured I was in enough trouble anyway, and, besides, when Cheerio dude said "touched inappropriately," everyone in the room knew he meant Tony J. Tony James has the fastest hands in Ramsey County. He practically has a permanent hand-shaped maroon-colored bruise on his face, he has been slapped so many times by all the girls he's felt on, and that is every girl who doesn't have a hair pick with a sharp point on it. If Smutts or any of the rest of them had done something about him in the first place, we wouldn't be sitting here playing the People's Court.

I sure don't want to look down there at Tony, because that would be like giving him away or something, but I can see out of the corner of my eyes that LT, Cool, and Demetrius are doing the same thing: Looking at him and not looking at the same time. Tony J., he is stone cold. Even though he is looking at his feet I can see his eyes shining a little bit like he is proud of himself that he is a human dog who can't even keep his hands to himself, and furthermore has gotten a whole bunch of innocent youth such as myself into a lot of unnecessary trouble they did not need at the time.

"We have all day," says Smutts. "Your parents are being notified of this incident even as we speak."

Well, Demetrius, who was always big and bold anyway and who all the girls think is real handsome, except for those girls who don't like him because they say he is too black, which he is very, (though it is always the girls who are as black as he is saying that kind of stuff) he says, "You can't call my mama, 'cause I ain't done nothing," and then I hear a round of me neithers from the other guys including Tony J., so I say something too.

"I didn't do nothing," I say, which is just the sort of bad English to send LaDonna and Marcus and Verda and Ione into orbit, and yes, I do know better, and I only said it that way so we could have sort of a brotherhood thing here. (Although as I think about it, I'm not sure why I want to be one of these particular guys, especially since one of them is a well-known sex criminal. But I did it anyway. I figured if you are going to be thrown in with the guys you are probably expected to talk like them too.)

Smutts just about pops a vessel, as Marcus always says he himself is about to do. There's one thing drives these A.P.s crazy is the "You can't call my mom" bit. Don't ever tell them what they can or cannot do. He slams his hand down on the table. He seems to enjoy that part.

"Listen up, son," he says. (These guys are always calling you son or mister. Unless you are Marcus, please, don't ever call me son, thank you.) "I'll be the one who decides what I do and don't do as long as I'm assistant principal of this school." He's got his finger all pointed in Demetrius's face, and then he flattens his hand and slams it down one more time. "I hope I made myself clear."

Some boys say, "Yes, sir," but I just roll my eyes. Like I'm gonna give him the satisfaction of a response.

And it's then, just then, he says something such as, "All you punks are alike." Or something like that. Then he goes on with a speech about how long he has been around and what all he's seen and how every time this and that and some other. Most of which I don't hear because I am still stuck back on the "all you punks" part. I'm thinking, which punks? All seventh graders? Anyone without a hall pass? Hell, no. What he means is me and these four dudes and then anyone else he can lump in with us. What he means is black folks.

Smutts finishes up with, ". . . and I hope you boys will just keep that in mind," then he gets up and goes to the door. "I'll let you know when we get the mamas up here. Then we'll see some action."

So there I am sitting with the boys and Demetrius looks at me. He laughs and says to the other dudes, "Well, we know he didn't do it." Like I was born with flippers or something and couldn't get a feel if I tried. But the boys don't laugh too long because LT says to Tony, "You just need to go on and admit what you done."

Tony slides down in his chair some more and pulls his hat over his eyes some more. He grins. He looks tougher than ever. He thinks he's really got by with it this time. All that toughness won't help him one bit, because what I can see that he can't see is old Smutts out there pulling back the curtain so as this new girl can point her finger right at him.

He was the one just like I knew he was.

Well, that would be that, seeing as how they got their man and justice was done. Except for one thing. At the very moment Smutts goes to escort us innocents out of the office, here comes storming in Grandma Verda and Ione. Just as I expected, Grandma is in the middle of a conniption fit, grabbing at her clothes and her hair and hollering, "Oh, my goodness. Oh, my poor sweet grandbaby."

"This woman here would be the boy's grandmother," Ione says to Smutts. He probably has this figured out by now seeing as how Verda has locked me in a bear hug and is sobbing and carrying on.

"Oh, my goodness," Grandma is saying, and this is such a scene that I bet I am the only one noticing that Ione has got all her Pentecost hair rolled up in Tropicana orange juice cans and tied with an old Smurf's scarf.

"Mr. Smutts," she says. "I am Dr. Ione Wilson Simpson. Just what has the boy done?"

Smutts does not notice the curlers because he is too busy looking at Ione's butt. She is wearing very tight exercise pants the color of swimming pool water. Marcus says those pants drive men wild—brings out the beast in them. Ione always tells him to hush.

It's just then I can remember who Mr. Smutts reminds me of. He is like that Barney Fife on Andy Griffith they show on TBS. Even though it was in black and white you just know that Barney was all the same color, too.

Ione says, "I got a call from a girl here. Evidently there has been some sort of a problem."

"Mr. Smutts . . ." says Ms. Marsden. Ms. Marsden is the little secretary woman.

"I went and got this boy's grandma and we came right over."

"Mr. Smutts, she hung up on me before I even got out the first sentence."

"Thank you so much Ms. Marsden," Smutts says. He herds us into his office. Grandma sits down holding on to me.

"Oh, my goodness. Oh, my goodness," she says.

"We've just had a little misunderstanding," Smutts says. "It's all been settled." His upper lip is sweating and I can tell he is trying to get looks over his desk at Ione.

"They accused me of trying to get a feel off of this girl," I say. Grandma goes limp, leaving met to sort of ooze out of her arms.

"Sweet Jesus," she says.

"Mr. Smutts," says Ione, "I can assure you that this is the finest Christian family I know. The boy's father is a respected educator, and I have just this morning talked to his mother from her cell where she has told me she is recommitting herself to the life and teachings of Jesus Christ. You have my personal word as a Doctor of Evangelical Studies that this young man was not feeling on anything."

"Mrs. Wilson, is it?"

"Dr. Dr. Ione Wilson Simpson. Dr." Ione straightens her back which makes her chest pop out even more. Smutts is bug-eyed. Grandma is sort of moaning into a handkerchief.

"We've handled this matter expeditiously, following routine procedures. These sorts of things happen in the course of the school year."

Grandma starts to come around. It usually takes her a little longer, but I can see she's done enough of her show. I can also see she is having some sort of a brainstorm. Whenever this happens her eyes sort of focus on the end of her nose and she gets real quiet. You can almost see the little wheels turning in her head. She puts her hanky away. (She always has a hanky ready for tragedy like this.) (There is, of course, always another tragedy ready and waiting.) She stuffs the rag back in her purse and leans up toward Smutts. "What made you suspect my grandson in the first place?" she asks. She is real suspicious. She might be crazy, but she is nobody's fool.

Smutts gets this indignant look on his face. "Every building in St. Paul has its operating procedures manual. As an administrator . . ."

Ione interrupts. She is standing with one hand on the desk and aiming a finger at Smutts. He cannot stop looking at her body. Marcus tells Ione that she has the best balumbas north of Chicago, and right now they are aimed right up in Smutts face. "Don't play jargon games with me *Mr.* Smutts. I have degrees in English literature and Religious Educational Studies from the finest Christian universities in North America. I expect . . ."

Then grandma interrupts her, "You," she points to me. "Out in the hall. Now."

So I go out and close the door. I always get asked to leave when the good parts start, such as when LaDonna and Verda really get into it. But I am not beneath listening at the door and I have learned excellent eavesdropping skills. I can't hear too much now, but I can look in there by pulling the curtain back. Verda and Ione both are giving him the old one-two. They are both ranting and raving and waving their arms at him at the same time. Smutts looks like he is sitting on a bed of nails and some of them are working their way inside. He is looking down at his hands and wringing them. He tries to stand up and say something every now and again, but Grandma sits him right back down. Every once and a while I can hear words like "heathens" and "NAACP" and my name. That little secretary woman tells me to sit down. I just look at her. I figure from now on I'll sit if and when I want to.

Ione opens the door. "Come on in now, precious."

They are looking sweet and calm like they have been in here having a tea party and reading passages from the Bible.

"I just want to make sure Ali understands our rule about hall passes," Smutts says.

"He understands," Verda and Ione say together.

"Very well," the big Cheerio says. He is being real sheepish now. He is all sweated out under the arms. I know he is shame. "I'm sorry if there was a mix-up," he says.

"Very gracious," says Ione sarcastically.

"Humph," says Grandma, walking out. "I'm taking him home with me for rest of the day," she says. Smutts sort of raises his hand as if to dismiss us. He won't even look at us.

I sit in the back of Ione's Lincoln, hands behind my head, planning my unexpected day off. I stretch out on the back seat. A couple of Butchie's G.I. Joes are tied together naked on the floor of the car. Grandma and Ione aren't saying anything. I figure maybe we will go to the White Castle, but then I remember that White Castles give Grandma the belches. So, I think maybe we will go to Mickey D's. But we just turn up Portland. As we pull up by Grandma's house she turns around and looks at me. She looks at me with a hard serious look. The kind of look I usually see her give to Marcus and LaDonna when she is asking them to please, for her sake, get a divorce. It's like she is mad, but it's not that. She has got something on her mind.

"Don't ever let them put you in a room like that again. Just get up and leave. You understand me?"

"Yes, ma'am," I say.

"Now tell sister Ione 'thank you' and go on up to the house."

I sit on the screen porch waiting in the sun where it is warm. Ione and Verda talk for twenty minutes. Finally, Verda gets out. Ione honks the horn and pulls away.

Plastic slip cover city isn't so bad sometimes. Especially when Marcus and LaDonna aren't here to fight with Grandma. All day long Verda is fixing me my favorite snacks such as Rice Crispy Bars and Country Time Lemonade. She lets me lay up on her couch and watch television. She puts a sheet over the slip covers so I won't get the plastic dirty, but that is better anyway than laying on plastic, which sweats and sticks to you even on a cold day in April.

At four o'clock it is time to go home and find some dinner for me and Marcus. I kiss Grandma good-bye and she gives me five dollars for being a good boy. I ride my skateboard all the way home and don't stop for the lights or anything.

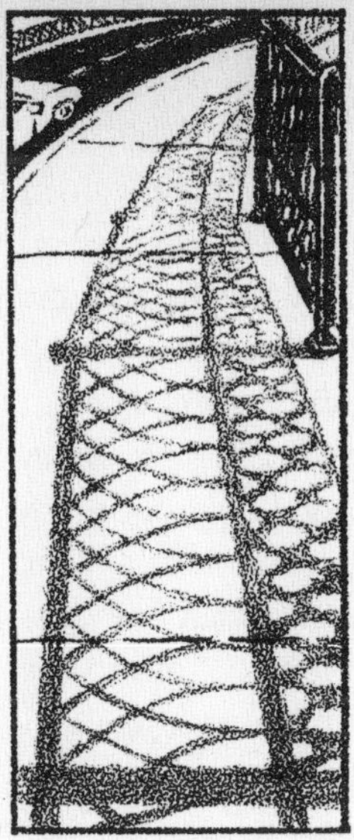

Verda

Verda can see them coming up the street. She tries not to pull back the curtain too far, because if she does that, they will see the curtain moving and they will know that she is home and they will keep on knocking on her door until she answers it, and then they will come in and hypnotize her and make her read from the Book of Mormon, and make her move to a western state where it is hot and her skin will dry out and she will be forced to become the seventh wife of a white man named Merrill who has a beard down to his belt. The other wives will be mean to her. She will be forced to wear a bandanna and do hand laundry. They will make her eat bland Mormon foods like boiled carrots and plain unbuttered rice. They will find ways to make her have more children: she has read about that—even women her age—in their fifties. She lets go the curtain gingerly, knows she had better be careful. Out in Utah those boys get special training for this sort of thing. They teach them Bible verses and how to smile and how to tell if someone is home even if she is hiding in the second floor bathroom. They teach them to ride bicycles and to be persistent. They give them a lifetime supply of white shirts. Verda thinks it is good that they make them wear white shirts because it's easier to distinguish them from your garden variety door-to-door salesmen or from homosexuals. She does not know if the Mormons are homosexuals but it is suspicious to her that they travel in pairs and are always fresh-faced and good-looking in a Norman Rockwell sort of way, but it is hard to tell about them since they wear white shirts instead of your usual homosexual clothes. But, then it was getting so you couldn't even tell who was wearing homosexual clothes anymore, since recently she had seen that nice young man Mr. Taylor from the next block over on Ashland wearing a hot pink shirt, which a few years ago would have only been worn by a woman or a homosexual, and seeing as how Mr. Taylor has a wife and four children he was hardly either of those. And even her son Marcus and her grandson Ali wore clothes sometimes which were only recently homosexual clothes, and they were absolutely not that way, thank you very much, and furthermore their outfits had to be excused because one had to consider their unfortunate living situation which involved a dangerous, larcenous, possibly murderous creature named LaDonna, who probably thought it was some sort of a joke dressing her husband and son like homosexuals. That woman had been a nuisance for going on thirteen years now, and although she was currently incarcerated in the Shakopee Women's Detention Center, she still needed to be dealt with, fixed good, forever, and in the worst way a person could be fixed, which is why it is especially unfortunate that the Mormons have chosen today to work the Lexington/Hamline neighborhood, because today is the day Verda has chosen to interview candidates to replace LaDonna.

The Mormons have disappeared. They have been admitted to Marjorie Peterson's house, a house that was once an acceptable shade of off-white with tasteful beige shutters, but has now been painted an ugly and ostentatious blue-green color that Marjorie pretentiously calls cerulean. Verda recognizes this as a color they have had at Sears for many years and in better times would have only been bought by people for use on the floors of their unfinished basements. Marjorie's is now the only house people notice when they drive down Portland Avenue. They go out of their way to drive down the block to look at it. It is notorious. There ought to be a law, but there isn't, which Verda found out when she called up City Hall to complain. And why was she even surprised in a city such as this one where they are too busy issuing permits for door-to-door brainwashing to be worried about upholding standards for good taste and decency. Marjorie Peterson would have never painted her house blue-green were her husband, Arnie, still alive, but since he froze to death beneath Lake Elmo (which served him right for being foolish enough to be in an ice house in the first place), Marjorie has developed all sorts of quirky behavior such as writing poetry and taking trips to Las Vegas and painting her house the color of a 1960s shopping mall boutique, and Verda only hopes that after they recruit Marjorie, the Mormons will find for her a real fat lazy husband with a whole houseful of mean wives. (How did they call each other anyway, those wives? Did they call each other something like co-wife? How did they decide whose turn it was? Why wasn't there more information about this on television?) Anyway, it would serve Marjorie right for lowering property values and for turning the 1100 block of Portland Avenue into the residential equivalent of Mount Rushmore. But, then it would be just Verda's luck that after Marjorie is whisked away to Utah, she will sell the house to homosexuals, which in a way would be bad news, because everyone knows how they cluster together and seek each other out and before you knew it, all the men in the neighborhood would be holding hands and kissing and who even wants to think about what that would do to property values, but on the other hand might be good news because as best Verda can figure, blue-green is not a homosexual color, and furthermore of all the persons she has identified on her A list and B list—A, being the list of persons about whom she has tangible evidence that they are homosexuals, such as their inability to use jumper cables, and the wearing of homosexual clothes before it became fashionable to do so, persons about whom she would be willing to swear in a court of law that they were one, and B being those who are real suspicious, the sort who buy French bread and do gardening on the weekends—none of those persons lives in a house that is painted anywhere near a controversial color. And if one were to believe Ione, those people keep meticulous houses, and one should always be a little suspicious of a single man who spends too much time putting on a nice appearance. That is how most of the people got on the B list in the first place. The main thing was: whichever list you were on or whatever your particular perversion, one did not trash up the neighborhood by painting her house a color that did not occur in nature, nor do any door-to-door recruiting for religion or for sex. That was the main thing.

The first interview is scheduled for eleven o'clcok A.M. Verda is unable to enjoy *The Price is Right* because the cord for her headphones is only two feet long and she has to sit so close to the television set, that she cannot see all of the merchandise, and every time someone comes on down it looks as if they will come crashing through the screen. But she cannot take off the headphones because if she does the Mormons will hear Bob Barker's voice and rush over here faster than June bugs to a porchlight. Today's first showcase begins with a set of his and hers luggage. Samsonite—a tasteful shade of gray. And of course you need something to put in that luggage so here is a sportswear gift certificate from Spiegel, Chicago Illinois, 60609. But there's more! You and your new luggage and your new wardrobe are going to need somewhere to go. How about a trip to Gay Paree! There was that word again. How was it that one group of people got to take over a whole word. What? Could a person just open up the dictionary to any random page, pick a word and say, I'm going to make this word mean something new today, because I said so and I don't care who likes it or who it offends because from now on it's my word and to hell with you. And of course they would have to pick a perfectly good word, which was until now in everyday use, a word like gay, and not a word like vicuna or seborrhea or dugong. They had to take a perfectly lovely word which had style and class, and now when a person forgot and slipped up and used it—such as saying we had a perfectly gay time at that party—you got funny looks and had to wonder what people must think. And when you've seen all there is to see in Paris, it's off to the eternal city: Rome. The audience oohs and aahhs. There is that same backdrop they always use for the trip to Rome. Two of the plastic prize models are dressed up as gondoliers. Verda imagines many people who win this particular showcase must take day trips to Venice, because, at least as far as she can remember, there are no canals in Rome, and therefore no gondoliers. It is a badly painted mural of the Colosseum and the dome of Saint Peter's. Verda figures they are up to about $8,000 on this showcase, counting in the first class tickets and week's stays at reasonably nice hotels. They have this same showcase about once a month or so and before Johnny Olson is over he will add trips to two more cities including Hong Kong, and the actual retail value is around $11,679, but of course the fat heifer that is bidding on this showcase will pass it to that dumb hyperactive black girl who got lucky on the showcase spin and hit the dollar and got to be in the showcase even though all she won on the rest of the show was a cheesy washer and dryer by playing the Hi/Lo game. If the dumb hyperactive black girl was smart she would bid $11,600, and therefore come within one hundred dollars of the actual retail value without going over and win both showcases, the other showcase, which will invariably include a car and Turtle wax, which is what the fat heifer wants which is why she passed on the trips in the first place. But the black girl is not smart, probably has never heard of Paris or Rome, has probably never watched *The Price is Right* and has just showed up for the show because her mama needed a ride and then, as is always the case, she is the one gets called to come on down instead of the mama, and here she bids $15,000, which is way over and everyone in the audience groans and Bob pats her on the arm and says "We'll see how well you do with that bid," and Verda yells at the TV that even that horrible dumb LaDonna could do better than that, which reminds her that she needs to be keeping an eye out for the first interviewee, though she doesn't want to get up till the end of the showcase round.

The first girl is late. This is a bad sign from the start. What was it with this country you just couldn't get good help anymore—just try getting your furnace fixed or your gutters unclogged. A person could die waiting. Verda has one eye out the window, and one eye on the TV. Today on *The Young and the Restless* Mrs. Chancellor, who is now called Mrs. Sterling or Mrs. Something-else-new, is being comforted by Jill, who is still called Jill. Verda has unplugged the earphones now. From the upstairs bedroom window she can see the Mormons' bikes stacked against the door of Marjorie Peterson's porch. Verda feels lucky today. The Mormons have been in there with Marjorie for quite a while now. She figures they are well into the brainwashing part, figures that Marjorie, what with her recent tragedy, should be an easy trick and should be on the verge of succumbing, figures the next time she sees Marjorie she will be as blank as a zombie, exuding happiness, already having packed her bags for Utah. They probably won't get Marjorie a bike. Verda has never seen a girl Mormon on a bike, wonders if she has ever seen a girl Mormon at all, except for that Marie Osmond who they claim is a Mormon but does not seem to have any of the outward signs of it, such as many husbands or a dangerous hypnotic stare, and as best Verda can tell is just another tarted-up country singer, and at least as far as she can remember from the *Enquirer* does not at the present time have even one husband. She must be what they call lapsed. Jill gives Mrs. Chancellor a hug. Mrs. Chancellor receives it tearfully. Verda yells for Mrs. Chancellor to watch her step. She has been fooled by this Jill too many times over the years. She should know better by now. Jill is a lot like LaDonna, except LaDonna is a black woman and Jill is not, and Jill probably gets away with more than LaDonna does, considering the fact that over twenty years Verda cannot remember Jill ever going to prison, whereas LaDonna has been jailed so many times Verda has lost track, probably more times than she knows, since, surely, LaDonna and Marcus have gone out of their way to hide the true nature and extent of her crimes. Well, she was locked up this time in the big house, on ice, cooling her heels, for weeks at least, and Verda planned to see that when she got out there would be a nasty surprise waiting. The trick was finding the right girl. It couldn't be just any old piece of trash because any old piece of street trash wouldn't be smart enough to do the job the right way, and furthermore, any old piece of street trash would leave things essentially unchanged, since LaDonna is the original piece of street trash if there ever was such a thing, and although Verda can't imagine anyone as trashy as LaDonna, one couldn't be too careful. As long as one had a job to do, one might as well do it right. Mrs. Chancellor tells Jill that she hopes this can be a new start for them. She hopes they can finally put some of their differences behind them. Ha, says Verda. Fat chance. Whenever there was a crisis these soap opera gals crumbled like cheap pastry. Verda knows that when the surgery is over, Jill will go back to her old ways and Mrs. Chancellor will come after her no holds barred. Jill will never change just like LaDonna will never change. Manipulative, money grubbing, man traps, that's what they were. She could tell the first time she saw that Jill, just as she could tell the first time she saw LaDonna. Uninvited guests: that's how this type always got in your house. If you were to for example answer your door off-guard and it wasn't Mormons or homosexuals, just your luck it would be someone like LaDonna or Jill who would just ask herself in and take over and before you knew it your life would have become a living hell and twenty years later you would still be trying to figure out a way to get rid of her once and for all. Or worse, she gets brought home by your own child whom you thought you had raised to have better sense than to drag trash like this in from the alley. Verda remembers to this day that Sunday afternoon almost thirteen years ago and how it was in May and how she had spent the morning cutting the brown dead heads off the crocuses which had already come and gone for the year and that after she put the ham in the oven and had potatoes sliced and ready to be baked in her special cream sauce, she had intended to drive over to Applebaum's to pick up something special for dessert, but had changed her mind at the last minute, deciding instead to put chocolate syrup over the vanilla ice cream which had been in the freezer for a few weeks now and would be a shame to throw away and had to be eaten now because on the end by the flaps was starting to get gummy. And it was also the second week she had experimented with Marjorie Peterson's recipe for Quick Bake Pecan Caramel rolls, which Verda remembers as having been messy and having involving wet towels and a Pillsbury product which comes in a tube and whose name she has forgotten, and which, despite the mess, turned out well and did oblige her to come up with a reciprocal recipe for Marjorie who back in those days lived in a normal colored house that she and her husband the ice fisherman had just moved into the previous month after which Marjorie spent a lot of time getting to know everyone up and down the block and assumed, Verda knew, that she, Verda, was a wealthy widow because of the fact that she had the largest and most tastefully decorated home on the block—if she didn't say so herself—and also had a son whom she had single-handedly put through the University of Minnesota and who would within weeks graduate with a degree which, even if it was only in English, would put him well on the road to a fabulous career which was more than the most of the rest of those slags around here could say. And far be it from her to set the record straight by telling Marjorie Peterson that rather than being a wealthy widow she was just a lucky one in that the day her late and beloved Marcus Senior was accidentally electrocuted in the automatic car wash on Snelling Avenue, both he and the car wash had insurance, his double indemnity life and the car wash liability enough to pay for the funeral, the car, the house, Marcus Junior's education and years of grief therapy, from which Verda believes she has learned that it is not the money earned through grief that makes one rich, it is the continued cherishing of memories of the beloved. That was something she had hoped she could pass on to Marjorie, whose quick frozen ice fisherman husband was also well-insured, but has been afraid to, what with Marjorie's poetry writing and her experimentation with outlandish exterior decoration. And now, of course, it was too late, seeing as there she was still, a half hour later, closeted up with those Mormons, who by this time have probably changed her name to Sarah or Rebecca. Right now they are probably boiling carrots for lunch and arranging to sell off all her worldly possessions.

The phone rings, then stops, rings again twice, then stops, then rings continuously. It is safe to answer.

"Sister Gabriel?" It is Dr. Ione Wilson Simpson.

"Praise the lord. I'm so glad I caught you in today. How are you?" Ione calls every day during the long break on *The Young and the Restless*. Since the heathen LaDonna has gone to jail she also calls in the afternoon, just after *Oprah*.

"Thank you for thinking of me, Sister Ione. Life is a constant challenge."

"Can you believe that Jill?" Ione asks. "What kind of a game is she playing this time? I swear that girl never learns. If she was my child, I'd slap some sense into her."

"Her kind never learns," Verda adds.

While Ione carries on about Jill, Verda goes to peek out the drapes. Bikes still on the porch. Good. Still no sign of the first interview. Bad. That girl was already ruled out. The agency only had three candidates in the first place, but anyone who couldn't bother showing up on time for an interview couldn't be trusted to do what needed doing. Ione continues yammering in her ear about *The Young and the Restless*. Today Ione seems especially indignant, though in the five years she has lived next to Marcus Jr. Verda has never known *The Young and the Restless* not to make Ione indignant. Verda worries for Ione. She is afraid someday Ione will have a stroke over the show. Back when Nikki was scheming on Victor she was sure Ione had lost it. She spoke to her about it, told her that God would not want her to be hospitalized on account of a soap opera. Ione listened. These days, to relieve stress, Ione rides her exercise bike during the show. Not only is she less excitable, she has, if that is possible, improved her figure. Verda has never seen a figure like Ione's on a white woman. Big behind, big chest, cute round waist. The sort of thing people used to describe as real assets, and yet, Verda always had to give Ione double takes when she saw her—and she saw her a lot, since Ione had decided that Verda was a poor lonely widow woman, desperately in need of Christian fellowship and therefore was always calling up Verda and making her go to lunch at the Baker's Square where a lot of Pentecost ladies hung out, or often just dropping over to visit after the class she taught at the Mid North Bible College. Verda would make her some tea and they would watch *Good Company* during which Ione always made special note of the Super Deals, but never stayed for *Oprah* because she had to be home to cook dinner for her husband Mitch, a bland, soft-looking sort of man, and their son Butchie, and Verda knew often also for her grandson Ali, too, because that heathen mother of his wouldn't cook a meal if her life depended on it. And on all those afternoons Verda would stare at Ione while she talked on and on—stare at her because there was something strange about the way she looked, something she could never quite put her finger on. At first she thought it was the fact that Ione wore no make up at all and had on top of her head a mountain of sandy blond hair arranged in loops and poofs such as used to be seen only in gladiator movies, except this hair was real, even if it never seemed to move, change shape, or require maintenance of any kind, save the application of a gauzy scarf whenever it was taken outside. According to Ione the secret to this hair was the giant size Tropicana orange juice cans and White Rain hair spray, which apparently in St. Paul was harder to come by than a warm day in January, and Verda had even spent a day riding around in Ione's enormous '73 Lincoln Continental looking for and was eventually located at a five and dime over on the east side. But it wasn't the hair or the face or even the figure, which Ione tried unsuccessfully to keep hidden in tasteful twenty-year-out-of-style suits and separates. It was only very recently Verda put a finger on it, and was yet unable to come up with a word for the thing about Ione which caused her to stare: it was that at any moment she expects Ione might stand up, snatch the bobby pins from her hair and go into a lewd strip tease. There is this . . . publicly sexual . . . quality about Ione, even when she is quoting scripture and praising Jesus. It fascinates Verda and scares her all at the same time. She hopes that when it happens—when she starts bumping and grinding and licking her lips lasciviously—they are at one or the other's houses and not in line at the Leeann Chin's Chinese take out.

Ione is still carrying on about Jill. She hates Jill, probably more than Verda hates Jill, maybe as much as Verda hates LaDonna. When she was allowed to teach her course on Christian Married Life, Ione would tape episodes featuring Jill and show them to her girls as examples on how not to conduct relationships. Since the state crackdown on the Mid North Bible College, Ione has had to pretend to teach literature and Verda has had to bear the brunt of Ione's wrath against Jill.

"Just look at her," Ione says. "Here she is supposed to be at the hospital being sympathetic and she's got on that dress that shows all she's got to show and more besides. What kind of woman goes to the hospital dressed like that? You tell me."

Verda starts to remind Ione that she happens to live right next door to such a woman, but resists since, for one, LaDonna at the present time doesn't live next door to anyone, except for more criminals like herself, and, two, Ione, for some reason known only to her and God, seems to find something endearing about LaDonna, a quality of Ione's character Verda would be hard pressed to forgive were it not for the fact that Ione, recognizing the dire nature of the situation next door to her, has intervened, doing much of the housework, the feeding of her grandson, and, in general, keeping an eye and ear open should real trouble break out. At least Verda sleeps well knowing that when the worst happens and LaDonna goes completely around the bend and begins carving up her son and grandson, Ione will come charging from next door to save the day. Or so she hopes.

"I tell you, I'm sick of this girl. Sick to death," Ione is spent. The tinkly music is on which indicates the long break is over. "One more thing before we go and I'll make it quick because I'm in the middle of all kinds of things for school, but that grandson of yours, and by the way he is the cutest thing on earth, yes he is, and I wanted to let you know when I was on my way home yesterday I stopped by the Kmart and picked him up a couple of new packs of undies and some of those big tank tops like they're wearing now. Oh, and I knew there was one more thing I wanted to tell you. I talked with Sister LaDonna this morning and I wanted to let you know how well she's holding up under her ordeal." She pauses and waits for Verda to say something. Verda doesn't. Ione is unfazed. "She says to tell you she knows you're praying for her and that you are in her thoughts and prayers too."

"Well," Verda says. It's all she can think to say without blowing up. "I'm going back to the story now." She hears Ione saying "Bless your heart" over and over again as the phone travels to the cradle.

Praying for her, indeed. Verda was praying for her that a big fat prison guard named Shultzie will slap her around and then throw her into solitary confinement and lose the key. Ione seems to feel it is her Christian obligation to make nice between LaDonna and Verda—always sending one love from the other. Messages of charity and good will, even after the time they had almost killed each other with steak knives. Verda would have cut her, too, she would have. Cut the cold trashy heart right out of the wench—it was her one big chance, really: the one good shot she's had at her—and, okay, so as she thinks back on it now, maybe she was just a teeny bit out of control, but considering the circumstances who wouldn't be. As it was, she had been up since six A.M. which in her calculations was the time you had to get up in order to get a twenty-five pound turkey washed, dressed and put in the oven so as it would be cooled, sliced and ready to be serve with the rest of the Sunday dinner at four P.M. sharp. And even though it was not Thanksgiving or Easter or any other major holiday, religious or secular, but just an ordinary Sunday in February, she, Verda, out of love for her family, was going through the extraordinary preparations for this special meal, which included peeling, boiling, mashing and buttering five pounds of white potatoes, doing the same to almost as many sweet potatoes, but then also making a pie crust for them, fixing the green beans, making the relish tray, opening the cranberries. It was more work than one person should ever have to do. So then she has all this food hot, on the table, and ready to go, at four, as usual, just as it had been for at least the past thirty years, and the heifer has the nerve to come sashaying in her front door at a quarter to five with her son and her grandson dragging behind her like they always do and then didn't even bother to say she was sorry she was late or boo or drop dead or nothing. And they come in all three of them and plop down in my living room and put their feet up and change my channel and start pulling out my magazines and reading and I look over and the broad has got her feet up on my mahogany coffee table which I had spent all morning polishing and didn't even bother to kick her shoes off. Don't one of them acknowledge me. So I figured rather than have a fit I would do my best to save the dinner, and a person does have to eat so I said, and all I said was, "There's food ready if anyone is hungry," and despite reports to the contrary I did not break down, scream, shout, or have a crying fit of any kind. "There's food ready if anybody wants," is all I said, and the next thing I know I am practically trampled by these heathens who are like pigs who haven't been fed in weeks. I have to wrestle my grandson's arm to the table while I say grace. He's got a drumstick he's already torn up, he can't even wait to thank our Lord Jesus for his food. And he and his daddy inhaled that food. Disgraceful, of course, my Sunday dinner is the only decent meal they get. That woman never feeds them. But her, she's got a look on her face like she smells something. She's sitting there reared back from her plate like she's afraid it's gonna bite her or something. This, a meal—

my best meal—I have worked on for the past ten hours, not counting the two hours the night before when I made the cornbread and chopped the vegetables and gizzards for the dressing. So, I dare her to say something. I say, as sweet as I can say it, "Everyone have everything they need?" And Marcus and Ali, those two having lived in her heathen house so long, those two can scarcely take a breath or grunt, let alone answer. But her, she says, and with her nose all turned up and with her lip turned out to the point a bird could perch on it, she says, "It's a little on the pink side, isn't it?" Well, right then and there I should have snatched her bald. But because of my commitment to family harmony, and knowing that I had cooked that bird till long past the little button had popped out and until the meat practically fell off the bones, seeing as how one can never be too careful with poultry of any kind, I said, "Well, sweetie, you must have just had a little cranberry sauce spill over onto yours." Next thing you know the heifer is up and on her way into the kitchen, *my* kitchen, so I say, "Excuse me, is there something I can get for you?" and aim to block the door but she is too skinny and fast and slinks on through like a snake. She's in there rooting around in my cutlery drawer. Grabs herself a handful of my steak knives and says "Poultry can be a little tough when its undercooked like this." Shimmies by me and starts passing out knives to my boys. They're on their second or third helping by now. Well, I lost it. Grabbed my carving knife to show her just how tender the meat was. "Now you look here," I said. "I'm gonna have to put you in your place now." "Don't be pointing no knives at me," she said, and she waved one of those steak knives around and bobbed her head just like the street trash she was. So I said, I says "This is my house and I will wave whatever I want, at whomsoever I want to wave it at, whenever I want to wave it." And went on to back the wench right on around the table, though to hear her tell it, she had me pinned up against the wall. Fat chance. I know better than to let something like her get the drop on me. I went on to give her my lecture about manners and breeding and about how she didn't have any of either and that just because I was a decent law abiding person she better not get the idea I wouldn't defend myself and my home, because I would, and that if she knew what was good for her she'd sit down and shut up and finish her dinner like her mama had taught her some sense.

And as Verda relives this story she can feel her face begin to heat up with shame. And frustration. To have let such a opportunity pass. She should have cut her then and cut her good. Sure, it might have meant a few years in prison, but then, on *Oprah* people were always pleading insanity and PMS and all kinds of stress disorders, and any jury in the world, or at least any jury in Minnesota, would eat up a story like this one. Two years—for God's sake she could be out on parole by now.

Still, there was more than one way to skin a cat.

Just after the noon news a taxi pulls up in front of the house. The Mormons are still up at Marjorie's. Poor thing. Verda checks herself in the mirror. Turns off the TV. Waits for the bell to ring.

"Mrs. Gabriel? Hello, I'm Doris Carter."

Oh, God, thinks Verda. A mammy type. Did I forget to tell them no mammy types?

"Come on in." Verda shows Doris to an overstuffed chair. Oh, God. A fat one, too. And, look: support hose. This wouldn't do. It just wouldn't do.

"Can I offer you some coffee or some iced tea?"

Doris declines. "You have a lovely home. Is this where I'd be working? I'm afraid the agency didn't tell me too much about the position."

Verda thinks fast, but can't figure out what to say or do to get rid of her. It had never occurred to her that the agency would send someone so . . . completely inappropriate. Okay, maybe they weren't mind readers, but she thought she had dropped enough hints, using words like young and energetic and experienced with men and boys in the house, and someone who made a nice appearance. It wasn't as if you could just come out and ask for a trashy, manipulative, homewrecking slut, who was also good with a scrub brush.

"I'm interviewing a lot of different girls for this job," she says. There, that was good. Call her a girl. What was she forty-three? Forty-four? She didn't look that much younger than Verda. Maybe if she insults her she will get disgusted and leave.

"You'll find few as qualified as me, ma'am."

Ma'am! Verda cringes. Polite and obsequious, as well. The woman gets up and examines the draperies and the top of the window frame.

"Your home is so well cared for," she says. "I take it you're losing your previous help?"

"The job is at my son's home, over in Tangletown, by Macalester." Verda lets out the big sigh she has rehearsed, which is then followed by her head dropping into her hands, all of which has been designed to elicit empathy and a request to hear what is so troublesome, and she has practiced so well that she is a ways into the routine before she remembers that maybe, probably, this one isn't going to work out. Not unless her son has developed a thing for large matronly women who were good with cleansers.

"Is there some problem at your son's home? I worked in difficult homes before. I got excellent references, if you'd like to see them."

Verda knew this woman's references. Sure, she'd worked for the Cleavers, the Andersons, the Huxtables: all of them. Decent hardworking American folks. She'd never done a job like this before.

"You see, it's the . . . mother in the home. I'm afraid she's had to be removed. I'd rather not get into the details at this time. Let's just say she's neither stable nor well. The family needs . . . I don't know . . . a fresh start?"

It didn't sound quite right to say they needed an attractive trampy distraction to make them forget that LaDonna ever existed.

Doris sets her purse on the floor, leans back in the chair and crosses her arms. "This isn't one of them daughter-in-law things, is it?"

Verda looks away. Had she gotten that transparent? She used to be so good at this . . . this . . . this figuring out ways to make things turn out the way they were supposed to. God: that sounded so manipulative and she might be a lot of things. But manipulative? No! That was LaDonna's territory. That's what got them into this mess in the first place. Okay, so sometimes one had to do a little proactive planning to make sure that things didn't get out of hand, but what was a person to do: sit back and let things go? Why, absolutely not, and just look at the consequences. Had she followed her own instincts and gotten involved in finding Marcus a suitable wife in the first place, none of this would have happened, but no, she had to listen to her brother, Thurmond, who said, "Give the boy a chance. Let him make his own way," and what does he do but make his way down to Conniving Hussy Boulevard and drag home the first little gutter snipe who made eyes at him. No siree. Not in this family. Thirteen years is long enough. She gives Doris a sheepish smile.

"Yes, well, I guess you could say it was one of those. One of those daughter-and-some-such things."

"Think I will have me a glass of that iced tea, after all," Doris orders. Verda gets her some and she takes a long swallow. "Now: Tell Doris all about it. I may not be your girl, but I just might have a few ideas for you."

As it happens, Doris is also a fan of *Another World*, but when Rachel comes on the screen, she spits fire. Doris says Rachel is a vixen and a trifler and people had just better steer clear. Oh, no, not any more Verda explains, and figures that Doris has probably not watched the show in many many years, and then goes on to tell her how Rachel's marriage to Mac made her into a new and different person, but it turns out that Doris knows all about that and has watched the show from day one, and the problem is she just won't forgive Rachel for the time that she sent Alice baby clothes right after Alice had miscarried Steven's baby.

"Humph. People say they change, but they don't. You stay tuned and see what I mean."

Boy! Verda thought she was vindictive. This had to be some sort of a record.

"What you keep peeping out them curtains for, honey? You said that next girl wasn't coming till three."

"Nothing," Verda mumbles. "Mormons."

"What you say? Where's some Mormons." Doris swings open the drapery and stands square in the center on the picture window. "Ain't nobody out here but some kids playing in the street."

Careful, careful, God almighty, Verda steers her back out of the window, Lord, all they need to see is someone standing in the window. She might as well have "Come and get us" written in neon lights across her front of her house. Don't you know those Mormon boys would be over here faster than you could say Jackie Robinson.

She peeks out again. Bikes still, parked, thank you God. Verda collapses on the couch.

"You're a nervous little thing," Doris says. She has popped her shoes off her support-hosed feet. On TV either Marly or Victoria is arguing with her mother. Despite the fact they give them different hair, Verda can't really tell the difference. From what she is saying she supposes this is supposed to be the bad twin. She has already spent fifteen minutes trying to persuade Doris that the twins are played by the same actress, but Doris is convinced that they really are two different girls. "They don't look nothing alike to me," Doris says.

"That trashy daughter-in-law of yours—what's her name? Madonna, LaTina—is she one of them Mormons?"

"LaDonna? No she's just a heathen."

"What's with them Mormons, then?"

"Actually, it's not . . . just them. I had a bad experience a while ago. With Jehovah's Witnesses."

"They hurt you?"

"No, you see I'm rather vulnerable what with being widowed and all. People take advantage of me. I'd let some in my house and, well, before you knew it I was going to meetings two or three nights a week and there were *Watchtowers* everywhere and then you know they have all these extra rules on top of the ten or so big ones everybody else has. And, not that I'm a heathen or anything that wants to go around sinning, but it turns out I couldn't even buy my grandson Ali a birthday present and so I ask the fellow—you know they don't have priests they just have these guys—I ask this fellow I say so you're telling me no presents at all, not even if they're in the twenty-five dollar or less price range and he says no, none at all. I said, "Thank you, no." Which would have been that except they kept coming by and coming by, and you know they were so nice and everything—I don't want you to get the wrong idea. A lot of 'em out there pretend to be nice, but all they want is your money. Well, the whole time I was going over there no one asked me for a quarter. And they always invited me to all their get togethers and things. I don't want you to get the idea they weren't nice. It's just, I felt like if I wanted to buy my grandson a birthday card or if I was in a car wreck and needed a blood transfusion, that God would want me to have it. But all these nice sisters kept coming by the house and just when I'd think I was out they'd drag me back in. Well, finally I said enough is enough. I went down to that court house and got me a court order and told them to leave me alone. You want to see it it's posted in every Kingdom Hall between here and St. Cloud."

Doris listens to this story with an open-mouthed gape. "Just when did your husband pass?" she asks.

"In '71."

"And you been living up here in this big old house by yourself since then?"

"I guess I'm just a pathetic old soul. Can I freshen your tea?" She takes Doris's glass to the kitchen. Something strange here, she thinks, this woman comes in for an interview, and first she's this proper maid, and now, an hour and a half later, she's got her feet up and we're dishing on the soaps, and I'm serving her tea and telling her my life story. Things takes funny turns. "You know," she says, handing Doris her glass. "Funny how we just met and I feel like I can tell you almost anything."

"That is funny. You put Sweet-n-Low in this tea like I asked?"

"Yes, ma'am."

"I said to myself when I walked into this house, Doris Carter, I said, this is a lady your dealing with. A fine lady. I been in a lot of houses and I seen all kinds and I know a lady when I see one."

"Thank you. That's very kind."

"Now: I been listening and thinking and the way I size this up, we got two problems here. First: you got this slutty daughter-in-law that needs dealing with. Had me one myself—emphasize the word had. We gotta plan for that. Problem number two: you need to get out of the house more. You done run yourself crazy sitting up in here. I been working domestic going on thirty years now. I've seen lots and lots of this. It's easy to fix, just takes a little coordination. Now me, I'm thinking, Doris, do you really want to get yourself tied down on another full time thing? My kids are grown and all out the house. Finally got a husband who works regular. Don't really need all that much. A little part time here, some time off the books there, and I should be okay, considering what I'm working for anyway is some spending change and to have a little set aside just in case. Plan I come up with is this: I take that part time over in Highland Park—another little Jewish gal with two of the sweetest little ones you ever seen—and all she wants is shopping, laundry, lunch and some relief from the babies every now and then. Offered me good money, too. And two days a week, in the afternoons, I come over here. I do your dusting and vacuuming and odds and ends. We watch the stories and then go out to the mall. Fifty dollars a week off the books. How that sound?"

"That cheap?" Verda exclaims. "Well, what if I wanted to have the bathrooms done?" Verda hates cleaning the bathroom. In the past she has tried to pay her grandson Ali to do it, but always found him sleeping curled up in the tub. Again, what could she expect?

"Tell you what: make it seventy-five, I do the toilets and throw in lunch every now and then. Deal?"

"What about my other little problem?"

"La-whosits? Girlfriend, shake hands on our little deal and the last you'll see of her is the screen door slamming her butt on the way out the door."

Checking the street again, Verda is alarmed. The bikes are still there, but Marjorie, who looks much unchanged, is out on her porch arranging the pink geraniums and the giant-sized marigolds, the yellow kind that are the same loud color as dandelions. She will keep those there until next month when the real ones can be planted. That's the other thing people drive by to see: the giant yellow marigolds and pink geraniums—dozens of them—all over the front of the blue-green house. Marjorie is wearing a white sun dress, that might have a pattern on it. Verda can't tell. She's got on a wide-brimmed straw hat to protect her from the sun, even if it is only April. Maybe she's killed them—the Mormons, that is. Maybe they got real persistent with her, insisted that she perform some sacred Mormon ritual right there in her living room —which used to be tastefully decorated in Scandinavian Modern, but God only knows what that looks like now—and she went off on them and killed them, but no, Marjorie's a smart one and she would know enough to get rid of those bikes.

The doorbell rings. Verda looks at Doris who is looking at *Oprah*. She can't remember if answering the door was part of the deal. She isn't sure if the deal is even in effect yet or not.

"I think it's them," she whispers.

"Them who? I thought you had a court order to keep them away from here."

"Shshsh. Keep your voice down. Not that them. The other them. The M.O.R.M.O.N.S."

"The morons?" Doris struggles up, scootches her feet into her shoes. She points at the TV and clicks her tongue. "You know, if I had done my sister out of her man I wouldn't be sitting up on Oprah's telling the whole world about it. I'd be too shamed. And the problem with you is your mama didn't never teach you how to do this:" she shuffles over to the front door, opens it and says, "Why don't you people leave this poor . . . Oh, excuse me, sugar. We were expecting someone else. Miss Verda, look who I have here."

In she walks, her black uniform crisply pressed, a little cap pinned into her short neat afro.

"I hope you don't mind. I'm a few minutes early."

She has the slightest accent which Verda cannot place. Doris, with her hands on her hips, walks around her as if she were checking out a used car. Doris's lips are pursed, she seems to making some calculations.

"My current employer let me go a little early. They's relocating to Chicago and had errands. I'm not going. Chicago too big."

Verda doesn't know what to say. She is the most beautiful young girl she has ever seen. Her voice is soft and high, and she has large round brown eyes like a caricature of a doe.

"You won't find no more hard worker than me."

"Jamaican girl," Doris whispers. Verda nods.

"I got good references. You not be sorry."

"I hear they're sluttier than rabbits," Doris whispers. Verda nods. She is stunned. She cannot believe how quickly a person's life can become something completely different. This morning she was a simple housewife, paying her bills, playing along with the showcase round. Now everything was different. It's like the day the police told her her husband had been electrocuted, standing in a puddle of water, trying to help some homosexuals vacuum out their car. What could she say? She could never find any words that made sense. All she knew then is all she knows now: things just weren't the same anymore.

"Name's Anne Marie." Anne Marie curtsies. "I start Monday, if it's okay."

"Monday's fine," Doris says. "If you got a shorter uniform than that, you wear it."

Anne Marie leaves, passing the Mormons on the way up the walk. "Not interested," Doris yells, and she slams the door in their faces.

One of Them Daughter-in-Law Things

I suspected there was something wrong with her the minute I laid eyes on her. You can call it intuition or whatever you want to call it. I just call it common sense. Some folks need to be hit over the head with something before they figure things out. Not Doris. If it looks like a monkey's butt and smells like a monkey's butt, I figure it must be a monkey's butt. Folks be wearing their problems like second skins. Don't get the wrong idea about me. Just cause a person's got problems, that don't mean they a bad person. Maybe that Lois Siegel's mama is, but usually they just a person needs some help.

I'm giving her my bargain rate: seventy-five dollars a day, though, it won't take but a minute to clean her place—she keeps it so nice—and it will feel like a vacation after picking up after that mob out in Mendota. I want you to know I'm losing money at this rate, cause if I got hooked up with another family I'd make twice that, minimum. The poor soul needs help, and she got me intrigued.

The reason I went over there in the first place was I had finished up working with the Siegels out in Mendota Heights. I wasn't the age to retire and I didn't feel like learning a new job, so I called my friend Deedee who runs what she calls a domestic agency out her house. Really all it is is Deedee has a phone and an ad in the Yellow Pages and then any of us girls out here looking for housekeeping work give her fifty dollars and she lines something up. That's all it is. Mr. Siegel, who was sort of an important Jew as I understand it, got himself transferred down to Washington, D.C., to do some political work with the senator, and he was taking the whole family with him, though Lois, that's his wife, she said she wasn't going to Washington, A.C., D.C., or any other letters and that all her family was in Minnesota and she didn't at her age need to be picking up and starting over again. She got a whole family as crazy as her mama is, and if she knew what was good for her she'd get while the getting was good. But, wasn't none of my business. This all started back before Christmas, "the holidays" as they called it out there, and by the time I'd come in the door at seven to get breakfast on, they was always already well into it. Doris, she says to me, this Lois does. Look at me. Do I look like some kind of a pack animal to you? A woman is supposed to pick up and leave her loved ones and move everything she owns every time a man takes a whim. Pack animal or no pack animal, when he dropped the keys to that new Mercedes convertible in her hands you best believe she loaded them boxes and got in line behind the moving van. Which is probably just as well, especially considering how their daughter, Jennifer Ann, had turned herself into nothing but a tramp, and had already as best I could count had seven boyfriends first semester alone and all of them the types you could tell wasn't hanging around her for the intellectual conversation. That there is all another story, but the point is, the whole shooting match was off to the nation's capitol leaving Doris in the unemployment line, and the sad part for me was I knew I was never finding another job like that one where I'd get paid fifteen hundred dollars a month for a little light dusting, some ironing and to cook a big dinner which didn't nobody but me eat anyway cause they was always on some kind of diet. So I took my references and severance and called Deedee and asked her to see what she could line up. First me and Earl took a couple days and drove down to Chicago. But that's another story, too.

I can't really describe how I felt getting up that morning. I don't know, I guess I felt . . . lucky. I felt like if I bought me one of those lottery tickets it was gonna be a winner. With things being slow in the domestic line, and me not wanting to do any hotel work or nothing like that, Deedee had only lined up this one interview. Said it was a woman at her church and she didn't know too much more about it, except the woman had a nice home and she was clean and all. So another thing that had me worried was I know what church Deedee goes to and I knew there was a ninety-nine percent chance that this woman was a black woman. I had never worked in a house for no blacks before because in the first place not many of us can afford to get help, and even if we did, I wonder wouldn't we be trying to hire a white cleaning woman. You know, turn the tables a little. But, as I said, things were tight in the job market and there wasn't a whole lot of jobs coming along and I'd already paid the fifty dollars and what with all the money me and Earl burned up in Chicago I needed to get something as soon as I could.

The house was over there on Portland, just up from where the rail line goes through, and I had assumed it was all white that far over so close to Summit and all. I drove over and parked my car and checked myself one more time in the mirror. I had fixed myself up real nice that morning, figuring since this was my only shot I didn't want to take no chances. I was still feeling lucky. I had put on my navy blue dress with the little white lace collar and the pleated skirt. I fixed my hair in a little bun on the back of my head. I didn't put on a uniform or nothing. You put on a uniform and then they think they can talk to you any which way. Mr. Siegel, he only made me wear a uniform when he was entertaining, and then only if it was business or politics, never for the family. Out there I wore a blouse and slacks, anything comfortable. They might of had a lot of money but they wasn't what you'd call fancy.

I get out of my car and it's one of those big old houses looks like it belongs out in the country. Painted all white with green trim. I'm walking over there and I can see someone moving the curtains back and forth and peeping and peeking. That was the first sign right there. And a more suspicious person than me would have turned right around and got out of there. But something made me go on. I figured it's probably just some old lonely person in there, and furthermore, Doris Carter is not one to make an appointment and not keep it. You get a reputation and you wind up out at the Rise and Shine Motel cleaning up after the streetwalkers.

My first thought when she answers the door was, hang on: this one of them bridge club ladies. That's what she was dressed like. Her hair was done up nice in that old-fashioned way, you know pressed down and kind of flipped up on the ends, and wearing a nice dress and stockings and this dress wasn't one of those pull apart numbers from up at the Dress Barn, no ma'am she had been out to Dayton's or to the Lane Bryant's for this number. She offers me some tea and I get ready to tell her a little about myself and show her my letter from Mr. Siegel in which he said and I quote anybody with a lick of sense would snap up this girl on sight no questions asked unquote, and it's right about then things get real strange.

First: I'm having trouble dragging out the details as to what exactly this job is supposed to be. I ask every which way I can but I don't get nothing. She sighs and waves her head and finally comes out with it. Turns out she's not looking for anybody to work for her. She's looking for somebody to clean her son's house. A mama's boy, I figure. And I am disappointed because she has right here a lovely home and wouldn't take a whole lot of work to keep it looking presentable, and it was comfortable too, and it sure looked like she could afford me. One promise I made to myself was I wasn't going into another rat trap. When I first started with Mr. Siegel they had been living out in that big new house for a year, and if Mrs. knew what a dust mop was you'd never know it from looking under them beds. Dust balls under them beds the size of cantaloupe. Took me a year to get that dump into shape. I was a younger woman then. I'm looking for something light these days. Like her house.

But, no this was her son she was hiring for, and knowing what I know about how men take care of themselves, I could just imagine, and I thought, well Doris, maybe a couple weeks down at the St. Paul Hotel wouldn't kill you. You made beds before you can make 'em again. But, Miss girl keeps talking. Verda, that's her name. Turns out, that ain't even the half of it. Turns out—after she's been hemming and hawing and I come right out and ask her—turns out this one of them daughter-in-law things. Well, I ought've figured it out right away, 'cause I had me a couple them wenches myself, and wasn't but one of 'em I'd throw a rope to if she was drowning. Turns out she's got one of the trifling ones. La . . . ? La . . . ? One of them La names. This LaTammy, to hear her tell it, has committed every crime short of murder one, and had got her son wrapped up in her clutches so tight, he don't know if he's coming or going. She says she done everything short of cutting this hussy to get her to move on, but she says you know how it is when they get their hands on something half way decent, they won't let go of it, at least not till something better comes along, and according to Verda her boy being a fully employed college graduate without a prison record, the chances that someone like her would find something else like him was highly unlikely. And, I know what she was talking about, too, remembering back to that one got her claws on my middle boy Chuckie. Thanks to Jesus she fixed her ownself without too much help from me. So I could sympathize, and I knew just how desperate she was feeling.

I made myself comfortable and sat there and listened to her some more, and then slowly I started to get the rest of the picture. Now I have been around troubled folks in my time—take that Lois Siegel's mama for one, and if she ain't plain crazy, I don't know who is, and why when they took off for Washington they didn't leave her in the state hospital in St. Peter I don't know. You can divide them into three groups: out of their mind crazy, plain crazy, and a little something wrong with them. This Verda goes in the last group.

We're sitting there talking and every few minutes she jumps up and peeps out the curtains again. She says she looking for Mormons. And then she starts telling you a story about these Mormons and it's one of these stories starts in one place and ends up some place else and you listen to it and you think it makes sense, but you know if you thought about it, it's just a bunch of craziness. That's how she talks. So I drink some more tea and we watch the stories and I do some more inquiring. She's nervous just like a little bird. Real twitchy and fragile. But underneath it all I can tell she's got her tough side. She might have been locked up in that house a long time, but you wouldn't want to mess with her. I know I wouldn't.

She's talking away and I'm trying to keep the thread of what's going on. As of yet I hadn't decided I would be working with her. Oh, yeah, she had a comfortable place and all, and I could see she was no deadbeat and would pay you regular. A person's got to be careful taking on clients. It's a big commitment and you wouldn't want to make a choice too quick. I get some of the details: she's been a widow for almost thirty years. Her main activities are watching TV and cooking Sunday dinner for her son. Some sort of Pentecostal lady takes her out every now and then. That much I sift out of all the rambling she does. That, and the fact she got all these fears. Fears, of a lot of different stuff, but mostly of people I think. I don't know what she thinks they want from her. If you look at folks like you got some sense and you know that they do too, they leave you alone. She carried on a lot about them Mormons—me, I never talked to one so I don't even know what they is—and a lot about homosexuals and how they'd electrocuted her husband and how she knew they were after her son all the time, and all kinds of ignorant mess like that. I could of told her that one of my sons is one, though he haven't told me and don't think I know 'cause I guess he thinks I'm too stupid to figure it out, and that my boy, Harlan, he been living with the same fellow since college and from what I can tell they ain't out for her son or anybody else except each other. Yes, ma'am, she is full of crazy ideas, and I have learned that when they are this far into it, you cannot change their minds by talking. You just got to take them out and show them there is another way to live.

I say to myself, Doris, here's what you do: take this on as a part time thing. Couldn't take more than a day a week to do this place and keep it real nice. Couple of times a year give it the full treatment—this joint would be a showplace. I figure that's half the job. The other half would be getting this sister whipped back into shape. There's folks might think all there is to a job is washing and scrubbing, but they be wrong. Really, when you be up under folks all day long and see all their nasty habits and ornery ways and the different messes they get themselves into, you would have to be stone cold not to have your say. I don't mean get in the middle of they stuff, but at least don't pretend like you ain't seen nothing. If that's what they want, they better just hire a robot. I figure with me coming in a couple of times a week and taking her out to various places and getting her involved in a few things, I'd have her back in circulation in no time. Get her out of this house and all the craziness she got herself wound into. I figure two afternoons a week and, like I said, I give her my bargain basement rate.

A while later that same day, we hire this girl. She looking for this girl to break things up over at her son's house. This girl, this Anne Marie, she is a cutie, but I don't know she is any homewrecker. Who knows, her son might not even be interested. Me, I just went along with it 'cause I figured it was her money, and this Jamaican girl, she probably needed a job, and, anyway, Verda, she seemed to be set on the idea. I wasn't at the point to talk her out of anything yet. Besides: I know a nasty daughter-in-law will run you right to the crazy house.

A woman don't forget daughter-in-law troubles, not soon anyway. It's something about letting another woman into your family that's harder than letting in someone else. For instance, I have this son-in-law Robert married to my daughter Renee, and believe you me he is no prize. But Renee is a big girl and a smart girl and she can take care of herself, and I know whatever happens he is not going to come between us, because a man don't come between a girl and her mama. But, boys are different, and I know myself that a woman needs to get a man away from his mama. I've gotten three of them away myself: you got to, unless you want to be living up under her shadow for the rest of your life. Not Doris. So when one of them comes along to get your baby, you know what the program is gonna be, and its your job to make sure if she's gonna take him, she's gonna do right by him. That's all you want, really, for the girl to do right by your boy.

Don't get the idea that my Chuckie was any kind of a prize either. I knew all about his ways because I had lived with them for eighteen years. He took after his old ornery daddy, was his problem—just as sly and mannish and about as lazy. But he turned into a nice looking brownskin man and he did go back for his GED and he keeps a steady job steady as long as he feels like it. He wasn't but eighteen when along come this Marketa, she called herself, one of them merhinny gals and if you put any more yellow in that skin you'd think she'd been sleeping in the mustard jar. She was one of them thought life was some kind of street party, thought all it was was you would go out carrying on till four in the morning, sleep all day the next day, have somebody feed you and then go out and do it all over again. She claimed to be going to beauty school, but the way that stringy mess on her head looked you'd never know it. Looked like the cat been sucking it. Mr. Siegel helped me get Chuckie a job down at the old Holiday Inn and he was doing good and making good money and then he met this wench. I don't know where, and I don't want to know and truthfully, there's some things about your children you'd just rather not hear, even if he was living up in my house eating my food. Next thing I know I'm getting phone calls at my job asking me do I know where Charles is. And I come home from work, and there he is in my living room on my sofa, wrapped all around this gal, and I go to get me a snack and they have eaten every damn thing in my house. I let it slide for a while. I knew Chuckie and how he was rather doggish like his daddy and he didn't stay with one too long before he got tired of her. A couple weeks go by, come to find out behind my back this little tramp has as much as moved into my house and I can't even find a place to pee 'cause she has got a thousand dollars worth of cheap makeup laid out all over the back of my toilet. I sat Chuckie down and I told him. I said you my son and you allowed to stay here as long as I got a roof. But I'm a Christian woman and there won't be no shacking up in this household. Don't you know the bold little heifer was listening behind the door and she comes out boo-hooing and sobbing about how she didn't have nowhere else to go and she loved Chuckie and her daddy beat her and her daddy was a white man, and them crocodile tears was running down her cheeks and dripping off her chin, and she was gonna have Chuckie's baby and they was gonna get married. And I jumped up and said "What," and then didn't want to hear no more, 'cause I said to myself, Doris, get the hell out of here before you have a stroke or do something crazy like kick the ugly yellow heifer out the door on her fat butt. As it was, I grabbed my Chuckie by the ear and dragged him out of there and threw him in the car and started driving like a crazy woman. Don't ask me how we didn't get killed, but the next thing I know I'm in the parking lot out by the lake at Como Park and I'm screaming and yelling and calling that fool boy every name I know of. And I tell him if it turns out it's true that simple ass girl really is having his baby —and we would be going to the doctor's first thing in the morning to find out—then he best get his suit pressed and buy the ring 'cause wasn't gonna be no bastard babies born out of this house, and furthermore start looking for another place to live, 'cause Earl—my third husband who is not his daddy—and me was too old and our house was too small to have a bunch of crumbsnatchers running around in it.

After the wedding I give 'em two months to get their things in order. I told 'em if they still there after that, then me and the sheriff would set all their mess out in the middle of Aurora Avenue and they could live out in the street if they wanted. Well that two months was all I needed to find out what a trifling little wench this was. This Marketa. She was the kind would take the wrapper off a sucker and then drop it behind the couch rather than lean up and put in the ash tray. She was the kind mess up every glass in the house, leave 'em all over creation, get thirsty again and then come all the way upstairs to ask me did I know where any more clean glasses was. I'm laying down on Sunday afternoon trying to catch up on my rest 'cause I work like a dog every day, and I hear her calling me. "Mom! Mom!" Now, I know what a difficult time being pregnant is. I had me four. In my heart of hearts I didn't want nothing bad to happen to that poor innocent baby. I get up, climb all the way up the stairs, find her laying in the bathtub with her legs all up in the air. Heifer says to me, "Could you please turn on the hot water for me. This bath is getting kind of chilly." Child, if it had been a gun on the toilet stool I would have blown her brains out. I had to get in my car and drive over to my girlfriend's house for the rest of the day. Don't even ask me about the ring in the tub. I get hot just thinking about it.

I know it was his own doing, and if he was going to be a man he was going to have to make his own way, but the thought of my Chuckie spending the rest of his life with this lazy cow was too much for me to deal with. I knew I was gonna have to do something.

Right on schedule, two months later they got their stuff and moved over to Chuckie's daddy's place. Arthur, he bought him a little bungalow up behind Samaritan hospital and was supposed to be living in it with some woman who was a practical nurse and her two kids, and if she was anything like me or any other woman I know she wouldn't be standing for too much of Miss Marketa and her mess.

For a long time there I thought about what I was going to have to do to get my Chuckie away from her. I gave that up. You know why? Doris didn't raise no fools. My boy, he'd figure her out. All I would have to do was point him to a few facts. He would see her for what she was.

She was able to run her little game right through till that baby was born. I fed them Sunday dinner all through there, and here she'd come waddling up the steps, holding her belly like she was afraid the baby was gonna fall right out. The bigger she got the uglier she got. She swole up all over, and got big purple bags all up under her eyes she couldn't cover up no matter how much make-up she plastered on her. She'd lay up on that couch and whine and moan all afternoon. Towards the end she asked me, "Is it always gonna be this hard?" I told her that the little mess she was going through now wasn't nothing. I told her to get herself ready for nasty diapers and getting up every few hours to feed it and to sometimes having to stay up all night when it was fussing. I told her that as it got bigger it just be other things to worry about: why wasn't they grades good, and who'd he get in a fight with, and what's that rash on his leg. I didn't tell her to save her strength for when she'd really need it, for when he brought home a big yellow lazy gal out of nowhere and started having babies with her right up on the couch in her living room. I didn't tell her that part.

It was a cute little old baby when it come. It got my eyes. My people's eyes. It's a little boy. They got them a basement apartment up off Lexington. Chuckie worked overtime to pay for all the things they needed. After a while he'd come here after work rather than go over there. I'd feed him good and drop little hints. You know: I'd ask him was things staying clean and did the baby need any clothes. Just little things to get him thinking. He was looking old already, like his daddy. He started telling me how Marketa was always crying and how bored she was and how she wanted to go out with her friends from the old days and have fun. After a while he said she really was going out some, and he was too tired to go with her, what with him working double shifts, and so she'd leave him up in there alone with the little boy.

I didn't have to say no more. Girl just up and left one day. Took the baby over to Arthur's and took off with some of her girlfriends. Chuckie, he didn't say nothing for about a week, but I knew something was up. He'd sit with us, me and Earl, till almost midnight through there, and when he did tell me, all he said was, "Mama, Marketa's gone. Daddy got the baby." I asked him what he wanted to do. He said he wanted to move into his old room, and I said okay. Like I said, it's a space here for any of 'em wants to come home. I called Arthur and he said he and his woman were happy to have baby Charles and that they wanted to keep him and raise him. Chuckie said it was okay with him: he wasn't ready for a family anyway. I could have told him that.

That's been five years now all that happened. Chuckie has moved in and out a bunch of times since then. It's hard for a young person to get started these days, but I think he is finally settling down. I hope. He has him a small apartment over on Grand Avenue, and has been working for the Federal Express steady for three years now. He likes all the people there and the way everything is organized. He has still not found a lady he want to stay with. Some of them it's just as well, but he has found a few I think I could have lived with. I think he's being real careful. He goes fishing with his daddy sometimes and they take the little boy. Boy calls Arthur daddy and I don't know what he calls Chuckie. I don't see him too much, considering the circumstances, but every once in a while Arthur lets Chuckie bring him over to see me. He is as cute as he can be, and I can't help myself, I spoil him to death. He calls me Aunt Doris.

Don't know what happened to that girl. I ask around about her now and then. All the people I know wouldn't know someone like her. I heard she went to Milwaukee at one point, but she has been lost track of. I worry she'll come back. Not for Chuckie, 'cause he was through with her long ago, but more I worry for Arthur and the little boy. He is not my favorite person, that Arthur, but he has done the right thing and he does not need to have her coming back here stirring things up. Wherever she is, I hope she grown up a little and learned a thing or two. More than anything I hope she stays the hell away from here.

I tell that story to Verda and she leans up and listens to it like it means something to her.

"Maybe there is some hope after all," she says. I agree, but considering the one she's trying to get rid of been around thirteen years, I don't want to get her hopes up too high. Seems to me if this LaGirl was going, she would have been long gone by now.

I look up and I have been sitting in this woman's house going on four hours. Here I had already promised Earl I would fix him a nice supper, which is something I have almost never had a chance to do on a week night. I'm still sitting up here talking.

This Verda will talk your ear off if you are not careful.

Dear Mr. Koppel:

April 25

Mr. Ted Koppel
Nightline
ABC Television
New York City

Dear Mr. Koppel:

I am writing this letter to you because I figure you are just as high as you can get over there at ABC. I'll get right to the point because I know you are a busy man and I don't want to take up too much of your time.

Here's the thing: we are a bunch of women locked up out here in Minnesota at the Shakopee Women's Detention Center. There's some stuff we'd like to get off our chests, as it were.

I know what you are thinking: a bunch of sociopathic broads, locked away from decent people like myself, because as a matter of fact, I myself thought exactly the same thing when they first sent me here. I wondered how I, LaDonna, essentially an innocent person, (more on that later) could end up locked up with the likes of this. In my weeks of incarceration I have learned that we should not judge people so quickly or harshly, and that many of the women here are simple decent folks not unlike you and I.

I am writing to inform you of several grievous miscarriages of justice. I hope you will be able to use both your tremendous personal power and charisma, as well as all the resources that ABC television and its affiliates can muster to see that these wrongs are righted.

The first case involves a certain Ms. Nancy Caldwell, who until very recently was a law abiding, upstanding citizen who I am certain the closest she ever came to breaking the law was possibly an illegal right turn on red (however do not quote me on that as I do not have evidence of any kind. Is this what you call in the news business a dramatization?) It seems that our Nancy discovered that her husband, a man whom she both trusted and agreed to spend eternity with, had been committing the most low and base crimes with their very own daughter. Yes! And knowing that you, sir, are a gentleman of the highest character, I will not go into the details here. Suffice it to say that the man is a dog and a heathen and deserving of the most rigorous punishment that can be meted out both on earth and for eternity as well.

To which prison, you might ask, has this man been sentenced? And this brings us to the greatest irony of them all. He is free as a bird, while our Nancy languishes indefinitely in the cell next to mine. In order to protect her angels from further defilement, our Nancy has sent them into hiding. She is in prison until she tells her husband and his lawyers and the judge he purchased with his more than adequate supply of cash money where the children are. Nancy is resolute and we, the women of the Shakopee Women's Detention Center, are behind her one hundred percent.

Mr. Koppel: We are asking that you use the resources of the ABC television network to publicize the case of Nancy Caldwell. We are outraged that in order to keep children safe from abuse, we are forced to send them away with strangers, into hiding, and that in protecting our children we are liable for prosecution ourselves. We hope that publicizing the case of Ms. Caldwell will cause an outcry and put pressure on the system to help her and all women like her. Please help unite this woman with her children. (You are our only hope, really.)

While we are on the subject of innocent victims. I, too, am one. Of: 1. The banking system, which, while being all too happy to accept your deposit, takes their own sweet time crediting your account, and 2. A Judge Cecil McDonald who works in the St. Paul courthouse and is intimidated by glamorous black women, and 3. A certain Kent Worthington, whose thirty-minute infomercial called "The Golden Triangle to Wealth" can be seen running on late night television, and who, were he completely honest, would warn you that in activating the Golden Triangle, there is a good possibility you might end up in jail. In addition to your work on behalf of Ms. Caldwell, please do a searing investigative report on any or all of the above named institutions or individuals. Since I will already have completed my sentence by the time you receive this and it will be too late for justice, I would enjoy the satisfaction of seeing the above mentioned caught in the act (on hidden video), humiliated, and then forced to own up on national TV.

We are counting on your help, Mr. Koppel. (Just a thought: If you have a choice in the matter, I would prefer that you not send that Barbara Walters out. While she seems like a nice person and all, I know from personal experience that the audience is usually busy commenting on the latest thing she has done with her hair, and often does not pay sufficient attention to the suffering of her subjects. None of us are too crazy about that Diane Sawyer either—she is so . . . blond, although Sam Donaldson will do in a pinch, and can be especially nasty and fun to watch when he has the likes of Kent Worthington on the hot seat.)(We enjoy Chris Wallace, Jeff Greenfield, and, of course, if you yourself could come, it would, in a way, make it all worthwhile.)

We're counting on you, Ted!!!

Write back soon.

Your friend, fan, and fellow concerned citizen,
LaDonna Brown (as in brown, and beautiful, and proud of it, too!) for Nancy Caldwell and all the inmates of the Shakopee Women's Detention Center

The Saving Place

It has taken all weekend, but Verda has convinced herself that just maybe this Anne Marie thing might be some kind of mistake. In the first place she has forgotten the story she was going to use to explain to her son why she has hired a cleaning woman for his house. The explanation either had something to do with a gift she had won for him at the church raffle or something to do with the department of health, but she can't remember which one, and neither seems able to be made into a convincing tale. Marcus and Ali would be over for Sunday dinner at four. She had to think of something before then.

And then there was the money. Affording an extra seventy-five dollars a week for Doris to come in and do her place was one thing, though that had certainly never figured into any of her original plans, but then adding on top of that another thousand bucks. The way she originally figured, she could get some reasonably attractive college bimbo for five bucks an hour. She figured: four hours a day for the three weeks it would take the tramp to seduce and entrap her son, throw that horrible LaDonna out in the street and then move on—she figured she could be out of this for somewhere in the neighborhood of three hundred dollars. A thousand dollars a month, the agency said this Anne Marie got, and that was for six hours a day, four days per week, and all meals provided. And no guarantee there still wouldn't be a LaDonna around when the dust settled.

When Doris calls to check in and to order cleaning supplies, Verda is well past panic.

"I really don't think I can afford that much money," she says.

"Think of it this way," Doris says. "It's a little more money, but you pay more for quality. This Anne Marie is a cutie. There's no way your boy won't go for her."

"Marcus is going to have to agree to pay half. How do I get him to do that? I don't even know how to get him to agree to have a cleaning lady in the first place." Verda has had little success convincing Marcus of anything, for a long time. Getting him to come across with five hundred dollars a month was going to be impossible. Marcus had, she knew, all of these ideas from somewhere that there was something wrong with having paid help around the house. Verda thinks it must be one of those leftover sixties things. Besides: Ione does all his cleaning now. "He doesn't even need the help," Verda adds.

"He takes one look at this sister," Doris says, "and he'll be needing some kind of help."

Verda hears something sort of smutty in that last remark, but chooses to ignore it.

"How long is this going to take?" she asks.

"These Jamaican girls are fast workers. Before you know it LaMona will be history and your son and his new wife will be honeymooning in the Caribbean."

It takes a few minutes, until after she has already copied down Doris's list and hung up the phone in fact, for Verda to realize she wasn't sure being married to a Jamaican maid was any better than being married to a criminal American nothing. She drops Doris's list, written on a Post-It note, into her purse and drives to the Kmart. She usually avoids the Kmart like the plague, but she knows she can get everything on the list there, and she also knows that if she is there, she won't be able to think about tomorrow, because when she is in the Kmart all she can think about is getting out of there as soon as possible.

One thing Verda hates about the Kmart is how they keep moving the departments around. If her memory serves her correctly, the last time she was here, housewares used to be over beyond the men's department. Now the housewares sign is hanging over by the automotives. Verda does not like to go by the automotives because there are always the sort of men there who have untrimmed beards and wear flannel. They always ask her if they can help her with anything, or something transparent like that. She imagines that there are women, even women her age, who do go to the automotives section to get picked up. Probably almost anyone could get picked up there, but she is not interested in that sort of thing, and if she were, she certainly would not be looking for love in the automotives department of Kmart.

She makes a left, deciding to approach the housewares department by cutting through the food aisles and turning right at the health and beauty aids. Not that the food department is without its problems. In the first place, why do they have all this food here at the discount store and what sort of person buys it? Verda eyes a shelf full of sandwich cream cookies. They are cellophane wrapped in stacks of three—there must be five hundred cookies in each package. The brand name is Big Bill's Freshest. Who is Big Bill? She has never seen any commercial for him. And look at the price: How can Big Bill afford to sell five hundred sandwich cream cookies for ninety-nine cents? Which is the other thing that drives her crazy about the food aisles at the Kmart. Everything there always appears to be so much cheaper than anywhere else, or at least you think so, because they are usually things you don't buy too often, and the price here seems like it has to be much less than the last time you bought it, and in such a large container, too. Like for instance here Verda sees a giant forty-six ounce jar of French's mustard for only $1.49. That sure sounds cheap, but Verda isn't sure. The last time she bought mustard was, well, she can't remember the last time she bought mustard, since she doesn't eat too many foods that require mustard, and it does keep. That thought convinces her she better get some now, because if she doesn't get some and she runs out and this was a good price she will regret not having done so, and even if she doesn't need any, it will keep, and if it turns out she already has too much mustard at home or this really isn't a good price she can always bring the jar back. And so here she is not even to the housewares department yet and has already spent $1.49 for something that wasn't even on the list. At least she didn't get Big Bill's sandwich creams. (Ninety-nine cents! She really doesn't know how he does it.)

And, so next comes the health and beauty aids, which makes her crazy also, not because anything is at such a good price, although, here, today, as always, are featured the enormous jugs of shampoo which as usual are parked out on the end where anyone driving by won't miss them. The shampoo is golden colored and the conditioner is creamy yellow. The bottles claim they contain things like jojoba, camomile essence, vitamin E, and something else called LDC-9000—a miracle cure for split ends. Verda imagines a person would have a hard time lifting one of those jugs and getting out just enough shampoo to wash her hair. She imagines that you probably would get more than a handful. But then she can see how the price would be hard to pass up, and would be worth a little loss each time you poured. Today the jugs are on sale for ninety-nine cents each. The same as Big Bill's cookies. Verda has always used Prell so she does not even have to think about it too much, but, then, what she does have to think about, and what everyone like herself has to think about in the health and beauty aids department—persons who stick with their regular brand no matter what, and even if Big Bill's is on sale for three dollars less—what really drives her crazy about the Kmart is having to think about things such as, do I have enough shampoo at home to last me until the next time I get to the health and beauty aids department, and if so, is today's price a good enough price that it would be better to buy now and have extra, even though having extra might encourage me to be wasteful, or, if I am running low, is this the best price, or should I drive across town to Target where it is sometimes, but not always about fifty cents cheaper. This is what you had to think about. And lately, all the stores have been marking almost everything as being on sale anyway, so, unless you went around with a little computer that had the prices of everything inside, there was no telling what to do. Feeling resolute, Verda goes through the health and beauty aids pretty fast and pretty much without stopping, except at the end of the ethnic hair care aisle where there is a stack of plastic containers in pleasing pastel colors that are really cute and only $2.39 each, and though she doesn't know what she will put in them yet, she knows she will find some use for them and picks a lavender one and sets it in the cart next to the mustard.

Thank God right across the wide aisle is housewares. She steals a glance down the way at automotives. There is just one of those bearded sweaty types down there who she can see. He is on the end of the aisle, pretending to price batteries. He's got on green flannel. As best she can figure those flannel shirts come with instructions requesting the owners not to tuck them in come hell or high water. Fortunately, this one does not see her.

She fishes the list from her purse. This is hard to do, because she must keep her purse hooked over her elbow to ward off the purse-snatchers. Ione claims she would rather have them take her old purse than break her arm trying to get it, and she, Ione, knew for a fact there was a lot of them would do just that: they were so desperate to get your money so they could buy drugs, they would just break your arm. Ione says that a person needn't worry in Kmart or in the grocery store because your drug addict did not buy groceries or discount items, but the places to be especially careful were in the high ticket stores such as Dayton's or anyplace where they sell rap or satanic rock and roll music, or even right outside your own home seeing as how drug users are most likely to be your friends and neighbors as anyone else. Verda thinks she would prefer the broken arm, seeing as how doctors and nurses were easier to deal with than the people at the driver's license bureau or the bank. It was one of those relative kind of things.

The first item on the list is sponges. Lots of those little different color hand-sized sponges. Just buy lots Doris said.

Verda does not like these disgusting little sponges. After you use them and let them dry out, they look like something maybe washed up on the shore of one of those lakes in Minneapolis. She doesn't know what it is you can do with a sponge that you can't do with a Handi Wipe. She herself only has one sponge—a big brown real sponge shaped like a lump of bread dough that she only uses to clean the bathroom tub. She keeps it in a Baggie under the sink. But: if Doris wants sponges and Doris is going to be the one scrubbing the toilet, Doris can have them. Maybe they can hide the sponges in the lavender box between cleanings. Maybe there is a larger lavender box.

The next item on the list is oil soap. Verda has seen this product on *The Price is Right*, but she does not own any, nor has she actually seen oil soap on the shelf in the store. She knows it comes in a bottle, is sort of a brown color, and even though she cannot remember the actual retail value, she does know it costs more than the Rice-A-Roni, which, unless there is a canned vegetable, is usually the cheapest item in the Hi/Lo game. She cannot begin to know where to look. Doris said that a person ought never put anything else on their good wooden furniture and that those Jewish people she used to work for had the same coffee table going on fifteen years and even though they had a house full of kids and had none of them ever even heard of a coaster, that that table looked like new and all because of oil soap. Figuring it must be with the furniture polish Verda wheels the cart to that aisle.

There are so many choices. All of the packages are day-glo bright, seem to jump out at you, beg you to take them home. Many things have lemons on them. There is a lot of yellow and Verda is overwhelmed. She wishes sometimes that everything came in plain white packages and all one had to do was look for the package with the right title: Rug Cleaner, Floor Wax, Laundry Soap. Instead, they put it all in here, all kinds of it, in a big awful place, under fluorescent lights, all crammed together. And unless you actually bought the Pledge and the Endust and the Spiffits you would have no way of knowing which one was best, or whether in fact, you had done the right thing. She wishes she didn't have to do this sort of thing at all. She wishes she could pay someone to do it, and then she thinks, wait: I am paying someone to do this. And if that's true then what am I doing here? Verda is so mad, she cannot remember the exact name of the item she is supposed to be looking for. She and that Doris were going to be having a little talk about this.

Verda wrings the plastic sheath on the shopping cart handle in opposite directions with her hands. And, just how did that woman get in her house in the first place? Seventy-five dollars a week, and for what? So Verda could go shopping at the Kmart? No way. She didn't need a cleaning woman in the first place. Why, she had done a perfectly fine job, an outstanding job, in fact, of taking care of that house without any help from anyone, for the past thirty-some-odd years, and there wasn't one thing this Doris could do she couldn't do and hadn't done for herself, and that included not only cleaning the windows, but putting in the screens and cleaning the leaves out of the gutters.

Once again Verda has this feeling. It is the same feeling she had when she found herself almost joining the Jehovah's Witnesses. Either she has been tricked or she has missed something. There she was, at a big convention of Witnesses, in the Civic Center, all robed out, in line and ready to get dunked in the baptism tank, when the girl in line behind her whispered, "I'm so happy I could burst. Good-bye world! I won't miss anything about the old life—not even my annual birthday bash."

Verda remembers thinking, that's interesting, maybe this girl thinks they are lined up to go on some kind of a trip or something—maybe into outer space. Just in case, she thought she'd better ask.

"You've canceled a party for this?" she asked.

The girl leaned over and whispered to Verda as if she were telling her something dirty. "We don't have parties. At least not birthday parties. I don't believe nobody told you that."

"You're kidding," Verda said. She could feel all the eyes on her of all the people lined up in the corridor to wish them well.

"We don't celebrate any holidays," the girl said.

"None?"

"Well, just the memorial of the last supper, you know, where Jesus says, 'Do this in remembrance of me.' That's the only one." The girl, who was maybe sixteen and had braces and what Verda thought were the worst bangs she had ever seen on anyone except maybe on a horse, was lecturing her in a way Verda thought was awfully smug and maybe even hostile. The girl took a deep breath. "Hallelujah! Today we leave the old world behind." She sighed.

Verda was shocked. Up at the front of the line, one of the brothers she recognized was ushering people into a tent. She felt herself sweating and flushing with heat under the robe. "Why didn't anybody tell me about this?" she asked.

"Everybody knows this stuff," the girl said. "You just weren't paying attention during your studies." Another drenched body emerged from the tent to applause. The girl shoved Verda along as the line moved ahead.

"I don't know about this," Verda said. "That seems like a lot to expect from a person." Surely, she thought, if there were rules about things like Mother's Day and Thanksgiving, there had to be a lot more worse rules besides. Maybe about things like the brands of perfume you could wear and what colors to paint your bathroom.

"Look," the girl behind her says. "This is not an organization for wimps." Her eyes were slitted, but glowing. She put her hands on her hips. "If you want to have it easy, you go join the Unitarians, or one of those other churches that Satan supports. Just remember that when Armageddon comes, you'll be sorry."

Verda didn't imagine she could feel any sorrier than she was feeling just then. "I have to go to the bathroom," she said.

Hurrying to the changing area, she had fished her claim check string from around her neck. She handed it to a lumpy, dough-colored woman guarding the baskets of conservative clothing.

"No water on you," the woman said. "Can't stand to look into the eyes of the Lord, huh?"

Verda was shaking too hard to respond.

"Always three or four like you. No spine on 'em. Can't face His divine countenance."

What Verda had wanted to say was that it had more to do with the fact that she already purchased fifteen pounds of Halloween candy, because if you didn't play trick or treat in the Lexington/Hamline neighborhood you were likely to end up with flaming dog doody on your porch. And there was the issue of the Thanksgiving turkey already on order over at Kowalski's. These were the kinds of things a person had to consider before undertaking a major change like this, and she, Verda, had not had time to think about any of them because she didn't know about all these rule changes, and whose fault was that anyway, since those nice sisters who came by the house two or three times a week for the past year had never mentioned anything about rules, and she's pretty sure she was paying attention most of the time and would have heard something like that. And she might go on to tell this woman, you seem like nice people and all and I had a great time, but, and don't take this personally, I really don't think I want to be part of a religion that would begrudge me a Mother's Day card once a year.

She didn't say any of that because she was trying to get dressed fast before they could rush in and drag her back to the baptismal tank which would instantly turn her into one of them. Then it would be too late.

"There's nothing out there for you," the doughy clothes guard said, and started quoting homilies about gaining the world and losing your soul, and rich men and camels and needles.

Verda grabbed her purse and headed for the Kellogg Street exit at a trot. She thought she heard clucking noises as she left the room.

Tricked, and left without all the information. As usual.

"Is there something I can help you find?"

"Pardon?" Verda is standing in the middle of the aisle blocking the way of a mechanical pallet full of detergents. There is something about the man's voice that troubles her.

"I know where everything is. It's almost guaranteed that I put it there myself. With these two little old hands." He stands very straight and tall and clasps those hands behind his back.

Uh, oh, Verda thinks. "I can't remember," she says.

"Is this your list right here?" He comes up next to her, plucking the list from her hand as if he were plucking the bloom from a wildflower. He is wearing a shirt which maybe is supposed to be white except looks as if it got put in with a red football jersey. He also has on red-striped suspenders, a little bow tie like the one Wally Cox used to wear on the *Hollywood Squares*.

"Let's see: well, in this aisle I can get you your oil soap. It's right back here." He strolls back down the aisle and his hips are loose and rolling, almost as if they have been oil-soaped. His badge says he is committed to customer care. Oh my God, thinks Verda. This isn't a laundry problem. That really is a pink shirt. He bends over, shakes his behind a little and sweeps back around with the bottle. "Ta Da. It was right down there all along. If it was a snake it would have bit ya."

And what sort of cologne is that, anyway? And why was someone with a neat trimmed beard wearing cologne in the first place.

"Thanks a lot," Verda says. She grabs the oil soap, spins the cart around fast as she can and knocks loose a pin rack of dusters. She hightails it one aisle over to where the Scrubbing Bubbles are.

This can't be happening, she thinks. She leans over the rug and room deodorizers, and can't quite get her breath. The room spins. She doesn't know if it is the concentrated scent of Glade potpourri that is making her faint, or the fact that she has just been assisted by someone who is probably the president of the Twin Cities Homosexuals Club.

"What's the matter with her today?"

Through her fog Verda thinks she sees a little Asian person.

"Verda, you look like you need to have a seat."

It isn't little Asian people. It is Marjorie Peterson and her adopted Vietnamese daughter Kelly MaiLee. Another reason Verda hates the Kmart is that it really is where America shops and you inevitably run into someone you know there and then have to think about whether they are the sort of person who would be immature enough to spread it all over the neighborhood, making a big deal out of the fact that they saw you shopping at the discount store and not at Dayton's, and if it is such a person you had to think fast of a good excuse such as: this is the only store that carries Fruit of the Loom underwear in my grandson's size, or they have an unbeatable price on sandwich cream cookies, and you know how mother is, if she doesn't have a plateful of sandwich creams at every meal, then life isn't worth living. She's ninety-six, and we don't want to take any chances. Marjorie, of course, is shameless. Every time you run into her at the Kmart, her cart is full of anything and everything. Today she has a cart full of yarn.

"Maybe I should get you an Icee from up at the snack bar," Marjorie offers.

"No, thanks," Verda says. Her breathing has almost returned to normal.

"You look like you've been running. My philosophy since my Arnie left me is this: take it one step at a time and take it slow." Marjorie is wearing a handmade knit vest over a man's oxford shirt and a pleated maroon skirt. Some sort of triangular scarf is tied over her blunt cut hair. "Live for the moment: that's what I say," Marjorie says.

Verda doesn't know what to say. She cannot believe someone, even someone such as Marjorie, would leave her house dressed like this. Even to come to the Kmart.

"I guess I'm just having a bad couple of days," she tells Marjorie. More like thirty years she should say. For the most part it was things like this: homosexuals, Mormons, tacky neighbors and their adopted kids. Thirty years worth of that was more than enough for anyone, thank you.

"Guess what?" Marjorie says. "I'm making rugs. Can you stand it? I was over at the Lexington branch library and I saw this new book all about it and it's the easiest thing you can imagine. You just hook this stuff together and they come out great. I'm making a room-sized rug for the screen porch. The theme is: Earth: The Living Planet. Hey, I could make one for you. Just pick out your colors." Marjorie tosses the skeins of yarn in the air as if she were tossing a salad. Verda had no idea yarn came in such colors. There are salmons and peaches and purples as rich as grape jelly. There is the same blue-green color Marjorie has painted her house, the one she insists on calling cerulean. There are skeins that are rainbows that are twisted together: beige rainbows and pink rainbows and regular full spectrum rainbows, too.

"She really looks bad, Mom," Kelly MaiLee says. Kelly has been building a pyramid out of aerosol bathroom cleanser cans. She is wearing a pale blue dress printed with tiny paisleys, with lace at the collar and at the ends of the short banded sleeves. She has on white stockings and black patent leather shoes. There is something about this child that makes Verda nervous. Despite the fact she is usually dressed like an angel, Verda suspects she is, somehow, dangerous.

"You sure you don't want anything from the snack bar," Marjorie offers again. "They make the best sandwiches. I eat here all the time. Since Arnie died. He wouldn't be caught dead in Kmart, God rest his soul. Now that he's gone, me, I say: Life is for the living. Seize the day."

Verda has suspected for a long time now that there is something seriously wrong with Marjorie Peterson. She has gotten stranger and stranger since her husband died. Being a widow herself, Verda knows that losing a husband is not an easy thing to go through—why, it has been almost thirty years since his electrocution, and still, not a day goes by she doesn't think of Marcus Senior and all the things they could have done together and accomplished. Marjorie's Arnie has been gone less than two years, and she is already like a different person.

When Marjorie and Arnie first moved down the block, Verda had sat on the screen porch and watched them unload their possessions from the moving van and carry them into the house. That house used to belong to Anders Lindberg and his wife Leanne. When Verda and Marcus Sr. came to the neighborhood, Leanne Lindberg had organized a door-to-door "Keep the Lexington/Hamline Area Clean" signature drive. That was back in the days when "clean" was a synonym for white. Leanne had rolled up that petition and stuck it in Verda's mailbox as if the mere receipt of such an important document would drive the Gabriels from the neighborhood. About twenty people had signed it—most didn't even live in the area. Leanne had gone so far as to picket in front of Verda's house with a sign that on one side said "Bye bye blackbird" and on the other side said "Send 'em back to Alabama." The closest Verda had ever been to Alabama was Gary, Indiana, where she had gone to visit her great aunt. She had no intentions of going back anywhere. Those Lindbergs were always bad neighbors: didn't shovel the walk, refused to contribute to the community council, had even put a chain-link spite fence around the front yard. They had moved to the new senior high rise downtown and Verda had been glad to see the backs of them.

She had been eager to see what would come in their place. You could tell a lot about a person just by seeing what kinds of things they had. Verda was discouraged. Mostly, what they had was junk. They had unloaded a lot of things such as beaten down old sofas and painted bricks-and-boards shelving. Even though they looked like they were around thirty, they still had the sort of things people had in their college apartments. This was 1979 and not even college kids had that sort of thing anymore.

The first thing they did, she and Arnie, was to pull down that spite fence. Verda considered that a good sign. The next thing Marjorie did was to go up and down the street and introduce herself to all the neighbors. Verda still isn't sure about that part. On the one hand it was nice to know who your neighbors were, but on the other hand, all this friendliness and insinuation was something that had never gone over too big here in St. Paul.

Marjorie told everyone that she and her husband had both gone to Macalester College—which to Verda explained several things, including the fact she wasn't wearing any make up (always a mistake for girls her age), she needed a hair cut, and was dressed like a longshoreman. She was a community activist and her husband was a biologist who specialized in northern spring fed lake life. He taught at the U and they didn't have any children but were hoping in the next few years to open up their home to a needy child from another land and that she loved to cook and exchange recipes and her goal was to make this neighborhood a safe and healthy place for everyone. She told all of that to Verda in one sitting. The first time they met. To Verda's mind it was too much information, but that was the way this Marjorie was—apparently, a lot of these young women were that way. Ione told you everything that was going on in her life. She didn't care who heard. She was another crazy one. It hasn't been just one visit either. Every week or so, Marjorie comes down and walks right in and makes herself a cup of herbal tea—she carries her own tea bags—and sits down on the porch or in the living room and fills Verda in. On who's doing what in the neighborhood and what they had for supper and how regular her period's been and other sorts of things Verda sometimes thinks she'd rather not know.

She has gotten stranger since Arnie died. She has painted the house a loud color and she has cut her hair in this odd square shape. She has been taking classes and writing poems. She reads the poems to Verda, sometimes. They are obtuse and mournful sounding. They have words in them such as "longing" and "chiaroscuro" and "afterglow."

She has become manic and silly. She is full of false-sounding good will and helpful household hints. She spouts more platitudes than a caseful of twelve-step booklets.

Verda does not know how to help her. Sometimes she is angry at her: for painting her house a color that does not occur in nature thereby turning it into a tourist attraction, for wearing dumb clothes and getting bad unflattering haircuts. For being always around, obtrusive, nosy and insistent.

Mostly she is afraid for her. She has already let the Mormons in and Verda certainly knows where that can lead. She knows how hard it is when you are alone and she hopes it is not too late for this woman. Maybe she can help her. Maybe they can help each other.

"Do you think I need a housekeeper?" Verda asks.

"Verda! Are you serious? Your house is spotless. Me, I'm the one needs help. Kelly and me, we're lucky we can find our way to the door."

Which is true. Marjorie is the sort of person who saves everything in little piles. Since Arnie died the piles are starting to merge. There is hardly a place to sit.

"I think I accidentally hired a maid the other day," Verda says. "Actually, I may have accidentally hired two maids."

"Oh, Miss," Verda hears behind her, and then. "Margie doll!"

"Dennis, sweetie."

Marjorie and the suspenders man hug each other hard and spin each other around a few times. He bends and gives Kelly a juicy smack on the cheek. "Good to see you sweetums," he says. Kelly says something that Verda believes to be in another language. She wipes away the kiss and rubs it on her dress.

"Verda Gabriel, I'd like you to meet Dennis Faulkner." Then Marjorie does something which shocks Verda: she grabs her hand and sticks it in the man's.

"Pleased to meet you," this Dennis says. "And, you, little lady, ran off in such a rush, you forgot your shopping list." He presents it to her with a flourish. "And lucky you: Everything else on the list is located right in this aisle."

Verda cannot think of what she is supposed to say. Kelly MaiLee is now standing next to her, her hands on Verda's shoulder, and she is swinging on her as if she were a gate.

"Dennis and I are taking a poetry class at the Loft," Marjorie says.

"Margie here is the most divine poet. She's a regular Linda Gregg."

Verda doesn't know who this Linda Gregg is. She wonders if Linda Gregg uses words like "longing" and "chiaroscuro" and "afterglow."

"Verda isn't feeling too well," Marjorie says. "I think we need to get her an Icee."

"Are you . . . Is he . . . ?" That is all Verda can get out. They all just look at her.

"Gotta run," Dennis says. "There's a whole shipment of sos pads in the backroom with my name on them. No rest for the wicked. Ta," he gives Marjorie a peck. "Toodles," he waves to Verda and Kelly. Kelly mumbles something in Vietnamese.

"Shall we?" Marjorie offers, and then lines up Verda's cart with hers. She begins pulling them in tandem back toward the center of the store. "That Dennis," she says, "is such a hoot. Every time he reads his stuff I think I'll bust a gut."

Kelly pats Verda on the back. She whispers, "No need for you to worry, Mrs. Gabriel. They don't bite."

Verda gets behind her cart and lines it up with Marjorie's. They go across the front of the store between the pharmacy and the health and beauty aids. Kelly MaiLee stops at the fragrance testers and sprays herself from four or five bottles.

"So many choices," Marjorie says. "Kelly does what I do: Get a little of everything."

Verda is somehow . . . moved, a little, impressed. Somehow, despite what has happened to her, Marjorie has maintained good spirits. In the face of tragedy, where others cultivated sadness, regret and hopelessness, here was someone who let optimism bloom.

"Stop right here, gang," Marjorie orders. She puts her hands on her hips. "Now: let's see exactly what we've got. She circles the deli counter as if she were examining a used car. "Personally," she says to Verda, "I avoid the ham and stick with the submarine." She whispers it in a conspiratorial fashion.

Verda is appalled that people eat the food in such places. In the display case the sandwiches glisten in their plastic wrap, looking like a pile of shiny, sleeping animals. There are already stacks of them in there, and a girl behind the counter is making more.

"You want the cherry or the cola Icee," Marjorie asks.

Verda just shrugs. Kelly MaiLee answers cola for both of them.

Marjorie slathers the three sandwiches with mustard. Verda wonders if it is French's. They get it at such a good price. She hands Verda the sub, a cola Icee and a handful of napkins.

Kelly rewraps her sub, but Marjorie begins taking enormous bites from hers. "I tell you some days it's like I cannot get enough to eat." Her mouth is clogged with food and Verda can hardly understand her. She tears off another large hunk. "Mmgoodm," she says. She is shapely still and as thin as the day Verda met her.

They leave the baskets parked and stroll through the stationary racks. Marjorie pulls out a card that is as large as a cookie sheet. A bald beige cartoon character has a line coming out of his head. The words "Happy Birthday" are at the end of the line. Verda has never seen a card this large before.

"You'd have to love somebody an awful lot to send them a card like this," Marjorie says. Behind them, Kelly MaiLee is snickering at a rack of cards that Verda knows to be naughty, if only vaguely so. Verda signals to Kelly and the cards, but Marjorie just shrugs.

"As long as she's reading," she says.

They stroll down the last aisle of cards, the end row, where they keep the odds and ends. Here are the "Congratulations on the Promotion" cards and the "Enjoy your Move" cards. There is no one Verda can think of who needs cards such as these.

Marjorie reaches out to a sympathy card. A gate and a dove are done in silver relief. She fingers images, pulls her hand away.

"Does it ever get easier?" she asks Verda.

"In a while," Verda answers. "Some days it does."

Marjorie chomps down the last bite of her sandwich. She has a look on her face that Verda sees as some kind of satisfaction. Verda's own sandwich is limp in her hand, like carrying around a piece of dead flesh, she thinks.

They circle back to the carts, signaling Kelly to join them. Marjorie sighs and puts her arm around Verda.

"You can take care of that big old house by yourself, can't you."

It is a statement and not a question.

Verda drops the sandwich between the mustard and the lavender box and abandons her cart there, between the case of submarines and the rows and rows of tasteless birthday cards.

Arc of a Diver

Jealous night and all her secret codes
I must be there on the telephone
I need my love to translate

Marcus has been lying on a cot in the sickroom for the past forty-five minutes. His students are at gym in the middle of a particularly violent game of trench. A really fat sixth grader named Rhonda is on the other cot. From his vantage it could be a large mound of dirty laundry over there, were it not for the fact that the pile kept swelling up and down with the rhythm of her breathing, and every few minutes the whole thing heaved itself over as she adjusted her bulk from one side to the other. She snores off and on, and it sounds like someone with food caught in her throat. Marcus resents having to share the sickroom with Rhonda.

Every five minutes or so the secretary, Mrs. Hooks, comes in to check on him.

"Feeling better yet?" she asks Marcus. She would lean over and feel his forehead, but even though she is fifty-seven and dumpy-looking and gray, and Marcus is over twenty years younger, she is afraid that because he is a black man, Marcus will snatch her down on top of him and ravage her with his king-sized black man tool. "You let me know if I should call anyone," she adds.

"I feel terrible," Rhonda whines, waking up. "Call my mom."

Mrs. Hooks rolls her eyes. Mrs. Hooks is ignoring Rhonda.

"Please, Mrs. Hooks."

"You roll over and be quiet. When Mrs. Leighton gets back I intend to let her know you've been down here all day and I don't see a thing wrong with you." Then she says to Marcus, "That girl! I tell you, if she were mine . . ."

Marcus wonders if they have a separate cot somewhere for the women teachers when they have cramps. He can't imagine Tamara Kartak lying here, moaning in pain, having to listen to Rhonda whine and snore and fight with the secretary. He wonders if maybe he should file a sex discrimination suit, wonders if what he has, whatever it is called, could somehow be construed as a male equivalent of the curse.

"Would you call my mom, Mr. Gabriel?" Rhonda implores.

The nerve, Marcus thinks. "Look at me: I'm dying over here," he says. He is lying on his back. Straight and stiff. A half hour ago his left arm fell over the edge of the narrow cot. He has yet to muster the strength to pull it back up. It is asleep now anyway, and he is looking forward to the tingly time when the blood rushes back into it—any stimulation at all at this point.

"Are you sick too?" Rhonda asks.

Marcus hates fat kids. In his experience they are always greedy, morose and antisocial, or, like Rhonda, just plain mean.

"No, I'm just laying here waiting for Ed McMahon to deliver my sweepstakes letter." Marcus tells her. He leaves out the endearment "you fat whale, you."

"My mom and I enter that every year. Ed's not bringing you anything because my mom and I are going to win."

Marcus has forgotten that sarcasm does not work on Rhonda, nor on any of the sixth graders around here. They are the most literal-minded human beings he has ever met in his entire life. They look up Gotham City in the atlas. They claim knowledge of a two hundred pound snapping turtle named Momo, which lives in Lake Como and only eats Hmong people.

Rhonda is sitting up on her cot now. She has made a new friend and has decided to be cheerful and flirtatious.

"You better get up now Mr. Gabriel. It's almost time for math class and you wouldn't want to be late for all the fun."

Drop dead, cow, Marcus thinks.

That's how bad things have gotten around here: Even the kids knew what a joke it was. Math class was the worst of all. Mrs. Leighton, the principal, has decided that every one—and that means absolutely everyone—in the sixth grade should be above the fiftieth percentile in math computation, even the kids his son Ali calls the grotesque mentals.

"There's no excuse for a twelve-year-old who can't add, subtract, multiply and divide," she said, and so now Marcus spends an hour and a half every day trying to get students—many of whom have not yet figured out what a four is—to fill in worksheet after worksheet after worksheet after worksheet.

"I didn't do my assignment, so ha, ha, ha," Rhonda teases. She is so charmed with herself you can almost see her eyes sparkling somewhere inside her puffy face.

Choke on slop, sow, Marcus doesn't say. What he does say is, "Join the club." No one at Hawthorne does homework, except for the little Vietnamese girl, Kelly MaiLee Peterson. Mostly they just leave it untouched on the desk at the end of the period. The good news is that Marcus doesn't have to make a fresh set every day. He just keeps passing out the same ones until all the ink gets absorbed into the faces of kids who use them as pillows during their third period nap and the numbers can no longer be read. Kelly gets sent to Hawthorne because

Marjorie Peterson has some quaint belief in the public schools and in "exposing Kelly to a wide variety of people." She turns in her worksheets faithfully and they are always correct: she has memorized the answers by now. In real life she is enrolled in a math analysis class at the U of M. She goes along with the charade at Hawthorne because she has learned somewhere—in some refugee camp or on some rat infested sinking ship—the importance being seen as just one of the gang.

"And guess what else," Rhonda says.

Don't tell me. Today is the day they slice you up into five hundred pounds of greasy bacon.

"Because I'm sick I don't have to take your stupid math test." She snorts and giggles and holds her hand over her mouth.

Marcus groans. Rhonda has never taken a math test in her life, nor any other tests for that matter, except for the ones given to her by the psychologists sent in once a year to discover what is wrong with her. She has been lying in nurse's offices all over the city of St. Paul since nursery school. Apparently she only gets up for lunch, to go to the bathroom, and to get on the bus to go home. She is rumored to have an I.Q. in the low 160s.

"There's nothing you can do to me either," Rhonda says. "I can do whatever I want. So there."

God kill me now, pleads Marcus. Before third period math, if it's not asking too much. Hawthorne School is an impossible place to work: the students are dull, humorless, and have the motivation of house plants. To get one to even write her name on the paper required the energy and entertainment skills of a Volkswagen full of circus clowns; an MTV video's worth to get them to learn that three plus five equals eight. Marcus believes it is something in their diet, that the buildup over the years of artificial additives, food colorings and preservatives has reached some sort of critical mass in this generation, and that now, because of some sort of unfortunate chemical/synaptical reaction, there is a whole country full of people who can no longer comprehend simple facts such as two times two equals four, and that gravity really is everywhere on earth and there are no exceptions and it doesn't have anything to do with how much money you have or how your arms move, and that it is really only the rare skydiver whose parachute doesn't open and who just happens to land on a haystack who survives.

Or maybe it is that they watch too much television. Marcus doesn't know anymore. After a day at Hawthorne it is all he can do to lie on the couch and have LaDonna massage his feet. She massages his feet and his calves, and works lotion into his skin so that it feels soft and warm. She calls him pet names like Sweetie and Dollface and Honeybuns, and tells him what happened on *The Young and the Restless* and about some ridiculous new scheme she has to turn olive oil into beauty masks. She sweet talks him shamelessly into making dinner, and if he has remembered to shop, he does, and if he hasn't, he calls Domino's, and while they wait for dinner, she reads him the news and corrects his student's spelling papers. After supper she lies across his lap and reads him a chapter a day, some days two, while Ali, their son, balls up in a chair or in a corner and listens, or doesn't listen, and reads his comics. And in thirteen years they have read all of Dickens, and John LeCarré, and plenty of trashy romantic nonsense. And then, the next thing he knows, the house is dark and they can hear Ali snoring in the other room and they are wrapped together and Marcus has lost track of what day it is. In the morning he is washed and dressed and packed off like a five-year-old, and it isn't until the Bronco drives into the parking lot, he remembers where it is that he works and that it is a living hell where he will hardly make it through the day. But it is only seven hours, this hell on earth, and, after, he can go back to the real world, to their life, and time where there is no time, and a pizza man is a sorcerer and a bottle of lotion a magic elixir, and tomorrow, if it ever comes, comes too fast.

Rhonda hauls herself up, drops her blanket, turns around and makes a loud farting noise. She drops back on the cot, giggling hysterically. Marcus thinks he hears the cot crack.

LaDonna has been in prison for two weeks. It is all Marcus can do anymore to even move.

The commotion out at the office counter is the kind of thing one associates with dog fights: a lot of thumping and growling and snarling. Marcus does not need to look up. He knows what is going on. His teammate, Tammy Kartak, the girl teacher who dresses right out of the Land's End catalogue, has dragged into the office Lamont and Santo, two of Hawthorne's most prized students. Tammy has them by their shirt collars and they are swatting at her and kicking at each other. She is trying to get them each to sit down on the little plastic chairs. Marcus can tell all this because he can hear things like "Get your hands off of me, bitch," and "I'll kick your ass." This happens everyday, regular as the electronic chimes from St. Luke's church. He can also hear the broken English of Kelly MaiLee Peterson. "They very bad," she shouts. "Get in big trouble now." When Kelly gets excited, she resorts to some sort of fakey-sounding rudimentary English such as is heard in movies like *Flower Drum Song.* She is often in the middle of many of the high jinks around here. If she has not instigated this fight, she has, at the very least, made book on it. She can often be found on the sidelines, egging them on and whooping it up. Marcus would like to suggest to Kelly's adoptive mother that she sew her up one of those little cheerleader outfits and make it official. He recognizes that this is what comes from boredom, and were Kelly MaiLee promoted to her ability level—which to Marcus's eye in the United States education system would be somewhere around second year law school—she would find more productive ways to spend her time. As it is she is considered Hawthorne's star attraction—teachers have been lured here with the promise of the privilege of working with her—and despite the fact that she is probably running a white slavery ring out of the second floor girls' rest room, she is, due to her Asian heritage, largely viewed as heartwarming and innocent.

Rhonda has oozed off her cot and is crawling over to the door like a giant slug to watch the action. She balls herself up in her blanket in front of Marcus's cot where she can get a better view. She turns and gives him an excited stare. They have gotten so close here lately, the two of them.

If Lamont and Santo are here, that means it is ten-fifty and time for math to begin. Marcus feels disoriented and disheartened both at the same time. He cannot face going back out there again. Tammy screams for help. She wants to know where Mrs. Leighton is. Mrs. Hooks comes around the counter and orders the fighters to their corners. For some reason that Marcus cannot figure out, children are deeply afraid of

Mrs. Hooks. All she ever does, to the best of his knowledge, is threaten to do old-fashioned things to them such as box their ears or read the riot act, and he has never actually seen her carry out those threats. It must be some sort of deep psychological thing—she must represent the archetypical mother of the soul, and they all must know—even the most hard core and jaded of them, like that Lamont out there—at some fundamental level, that if they cross her, it's extra chores, no dessert and intense and penetrating guilt for eternity. Why else would they be out there now cowering in front of a short, dumpy woman in a polyester double-knit pantsuit?

Tammy stomps into the nurses' station and with her foot sweeps Rhonda away from in front of Marcus.

"Shoo," Tammy says. Rhonda rolls away, but just a few inches. She gives Tammy the same look a pit bull might give a rattlesnake. Tammy pointedly squares her back, turns from Rhonda and puffs her cheeks out in a crude imitation. Behind her back Rhonda does the same thing.

Marcus cannot believe this is happening to him. He is still prostrate, his arm as dead as stone.

Tammy is hot. "Damn black kids at this school," she says. "Send every one of them straight to the electric chair for all I care. Save the taxpayers some money."

Tammy forgets, or perhaps has as yet to notice that Marcus is also a black person. Today Tammy is wearing the Land's End knit polo shirt in the royal blue, and the beige cotton twill pants featured on the cover of the March catalog. Marcus has lost count of the horrible things Tammy has said about blacks. At the drop of a hat she is ready to supply commentary and supporting bogus statistical information about African-American hygiene, musical tastes, sexual mores and intelligence. She has even used the N word.

"If we could just get rid of about half of them, this school would be a decent place," she says to Marcus. "Did you know this Lamont has a brother in kindergarten? They says he's worse than this one, if you can imagine that. If he lives to sixth grade, you get him. I'm not teaching any more of them. Not if I can help it."

Marcus does not respond. Despite the fact they are teammates, he has almost never said anything to her except for things like "I'm on page fifty-four" and "I'll teach all the math if you teach all the reading." Most people would recognize they were being ignored, but not Tammy. She reads his silence as acquiescence, his wooden face as permission. His colleagues—and it pains him to have to call them that—either tolerate her or consider her a harmless crank. There are a lot of lonely women in this profession, and many of them are pleased to have a cheerful lunch partner or a drinking buddy, even if she is the biggest bigot this side of Alabama.

Marcus also knows that any number of his colleagues agree with her.

At first he thought he should front her off. Maybe sit her down and tell her she was ignorant and wrong and that he didn't like listening to that kind of stuff and he wouldn't tolerate it in front of the kids. LaDonna—who is world-wise, wily and, above all, suspicious—advised against this approach. LaDonna said that she knew the type and that he'd better be careful, because if he said anything to her, next thing you knew it would come out that he had tried to feel her up and then he would be the one up shit creek. Just write it all down, LaDonna said, and for a while there he did. Until it got absurd and redundant and pointless. Keeping track of Tamara's racial trash was like pulling fleas off a yard dog—as fast as you pulled, there was another one to take its place.

She covers it all up with this phony and bubbly personality, just like the plastic prize models on *The Price is Right*, a show neither his wife nor his mother has missed for the past ten years. She giggles and bounces her ponytail around and whispers with the girls in the teachers' lounge. Sometimes it was more like a sorority in there than a school lunchroom.

He reported her once. Once, last year, after in front of her class she called one of her students a big black baboon. He went to Mrs. Leighton and told her. Mrs. Leighton's first response had been to shrug. That was her response to a lot of things—to when there was a fight or when someone lost control of the class or when there was no more paper to copy the worksheets that she demanded they use: shrug. The only things she got excited about were things that might wind up in the paper, things such as test scores or child abuse charges, things that might affect *her* career. The St. Paul paper didn't care about racism: half the reporters there were as bad as Tamara, and he knew that because his best friend worked there.

Mrs. Leighton shrugged and Marcus was taken aback, but only for a minute. So he told the story again. Today, one of Ms. Kartak's students was up yelling at someone across the room and she called him a big black baboon and told him to sit down. He told Mrs. Leighton that he had heard a lot of those kinds of racial things from her in the past, and that he didn't think it was appropriate in the school setting.

"Oh," was Mrs. Leighton's next comment, and then she went into a spiel about how this was a very delicate situation and if he wanted to pursue it a lot of people would need to be gotten involved including perhaps attorneys and the union and these were serious charges and they could certainly affect that young woman's career and that she would be happy to provide him with the forms to get the process started as long as he was aware of the seriousness before he went into it.

In other words, she dumped it all back on him.

That night LaDonna had made him a bubble bath and filled the bathroom with candles and opened a bottle of wine. She had nestled him against her in the tub and ran her soapy fingers around his chest and massaged his neck and shoulders.

"She'll get hers one of these days," LaDonna had said. Which was the sort of thing LaDonna believed. She believed in spells and hexes and all manner of cosmic justice. She believed in the Big Wheel that turned, and whatever you put on it came back around doubled next time.

And she has been in jail two weeks now because of what she believes, and here this Tammy is standing over him, glowering and grimacing. She pulls her hair back in a ponytail so tight her eyes take on an almond shape. Marcus cannot imagine she does this on her own. He imagines her husband behind her on the bed, knee in her back, pulling that hair back hard as hard as he can, fixing her good for being the ball-breaker she is.

"Time for math," she says. "If you think I'm going up there without you, you're crazy."

Marcus knows why, too. If it weren't for him, they would kill her. The students would. Which, after all, was the terrible irony here: through some twisted joke of a circumstance Marcus has become her protection at Hawthorne. Somehow, and in some way he didn't quite understand, for those black kids and for their families, having Mr. Gabriel there meant Ms. Kartak could be tolerated. At least up to a point, and through whatever shrewdness, Tamara has managed to just avoid crossing the line for going on three years now. As much as Marcus has hoped she'd put her big mouth right in it, she seemed to know just when to quit. Even when she'd said the N word, she'd sort of whispered it, as part of conversation he had no right to be overhearing, and she said it in a way that, if challenged, she could have claimed she had said nigra or niggardly or Schwartzenegger for that matter.

"Get up and let's go," Tammy orders. "You, too," she says to Rhonda. Rhonda gives her the finger. For a minute Marcus likes Rhonda a little better. But only for a minute.

Kelly MaiLee Peterson is behind Marcus pushing him down the corridor toward math class.

"Come on, old man," she says. "We got more worksheet to pass out. Us boys and girls can hardly wait. This best part of day."

His legs feel like lead, and the arm he anticipated would tingle burns as if set on fire.

"You move like worn out man. If wife not in jail, think she wear you out again."

For a twelve-year-old, Kelly MaiLee is rather sophisticated. In fact, Marcus does not believe Kelly MaiLee is twelve at all. He guesses her age to be somewhere between seventeen and twenty-four, but her adoptive mother, Marjorie, insists that when she picked Kelly MaiLee up at the airport five years ago, she received a notarized letter proving she was really seven. At home she is as sweet as a sitcom princess. All over the house there are pictures of her with toothy simpering smiles.

Two tiny Asian boys scurry by in the hall. Marcus does not know where they are from. They are holding hands and weary guilty grins. Kelly MaiLee yabbers at them in a language Marcus does not recognize.

"Those two very bad. Make nasty nasty in hall."

"Give it a rest with the pidgin English," Marcus orders. Kelly, who is also enrolled in a Shakespeare class at the U, probably speaks better English than Queen Elizabeth.

She says, " Big American G.I. like all us girl speak funny ha ha. Do naughty naughty boom boom."

Marcus can't imagine what Kelly MaiLee could possibly know about big American G.I.s, and truthfully, he doesn't want to think about it. He has tried to talk to Marjorie about Kelly, but has never gotten too far. On conference night he told her that he thought Kelly acted a little too mature for her age and that he was afraid people got the wrong idea about her. Marjorie Peterson was the kind of parent who wrote down everything you said to her, word for word, and then read it back to you. She read back to him what he had said about Kelly and then asked him if there was anything else. He said no, and then Marjorie said, "Well, that's one person's opinion," and left. That made him nervous, to the point he even asked Kelly what her mother did with those notebooks. She said they were her mother's poetry journals, and that every once and a while she went through them and made the things people said to her into her famous found poems. Kelly claimed that the poems were really good and that the literary magazines couldn't snap them up fast enough. Marcus's mother Verda says that you have to forgive Marjorie because she has not been right since her husband Arnie died in a bizarre ice house accident. And, he would have thought Kelly would be sensitive about that, seeing as how Arnie had been her adoptive dad for three years at the time, but it seems she enjoys telling the story. Marcus has found her with a whole group of children gathered round, telling all the gory details—details that she has to be making up, because she wasn't there and couldn't possibly know. She especially liked to describe how the super space heater Arnie had designed was glowing red as it melted through the ice, and how it must have been two hundred degrees in the ice house, and how he went in after it and froze almost instantly in the chill January lake waters. "Mr. Corningware," she calls him. "From oven to freezer in no time flat."

Which is the real thing Marcus cannot figure out how to tell Marjorie: how tasteless her daughter sometimes is. He just can't think of any way to say it tactfully.

Kelly MaiLee shoves Marcus in the door in front of her. She flashes the lights on and off about six times.

"All right boys and girls. Settle down in here," she orders.

It always surprises Marcus when they listen to her, and most of them settle down and face forward. They have just returned from their gym class. They are dripping and sweaty and the room smells like socks and onions. He has given up lecturing on deodorant with this crew. He can't imagine going around smelling the way some of them did. When he was a kid, no one would ever go around other kids smelling like a wet dog. He considers this another key indicator that in real life America—as opposed to TV life or political life or what people-who-decide-what-school-is-supposed-to-be-like-for-kids life—in *real* life, things had fundamentally changed, and the world was a radically different place than you might believe it was. Someday, when there was time and he wasn't so tired he was going to develop a whole theory about this.

"Chair for Mr. Gabriel," Kelly orders. Danny Vincent, the class suckup, runs over with Marcus's chair. Kelly seats him and Danny pushes him to his desk. Kelly goes to the back corner to settle down a group of the larger boys who are still talking loudly about today's trench game.

"I blasted your face off with the ball," Cedric says.

"Nigger, that ball didn't even come near me," says Mario.

Trench is a game, the point of which, as far as Marcus can figure, is to use a large red rubber ball to maim or cripple members of the opposing team. So far this year there have been four broken fingers, a concussion, several disfigured noses, and any number of black eyes. Fortunately, it was April and the heart of the trench season had passed. Mr. Rentucci, the phy. ed. teacher, has tried to teach other indoor games, but to no avail. It is well-known throughout the city that Hawthorne students will only play basketball and trench. It is a sort of specialty here, the same way other schools specialize in Spanish or in the arts. Marcus thinks it is a shame that there is no Olympic event in trench. In addition to allowing the U.S. to humiliate a lot of those mild-mannered European nations, it would increase exponentially the employment opportunities for Hawthorne graduates, who, after retiring from the professional trench league could go on to coach trench at the college level.

He recommends it be part of the winter games where there are not many sports that African-Americans do well in.

"Who won today?" Marcus asks.

"Boyz in the Hood," Danny answers.

"Again," Marcus says. He rolls his eyes. There are two sixth grade trench teams. Boyz in the Hood and Guns 'n' Roses. They are segregated. So far the score for the year is Boyz in the Hood: 97, Guns 'n' Roses 3. Guns won their three games the week Cedric and Mario and Leesha, who is the queen of trench, were out simultaneously with the flu. Tammy Kartak believes there is a genetic basis for the success of Boyz in the Hood, and she feels that trench is a valuable lesson in life for the students on the Guns 'n' Roses team.

"What you learn is that you can't be too careful around them," she says. "Me, I lock my car doors whenever I even get close to *that* neighborhood."

Marcus wanted to tell her that statistically she is safer in *that* neighborhood than where she lives, out in North St. Paul—the unwed mothers' capital of the Midwest—but he didn't.

Kelly has her hands on her hips and is sassing the big boys. One of them says something and they all let out what Marcus hears as very lewd laughs. She slaps their faces playfully and to Marcus's relief they sit down.

"Clean off desks for math test," Kelly orders. Those who are not already napping sweep whatever is on their desks to the floor. Once on the floor it becomes community property—that is common knowledge. The custodian sweeps once a week. Between times things pile up and fester, something like at the slaughter house.

"He still messed up?" Quinta asks. Quinta is a large black girl who once drove the school bus home after the driver blacked out.

"He not do too good," Kelly said. "Wife still in jail. Not get any . . ." and then she made a gesture sticking the forefinger of one hand through a loop made by the other.

"You didn't just do what I think you just did?" Marcus asks.

"What? No! Me simple girl from village. Just off boat. No understand."

"Come here." Marcus gestures with his finger. "Come closer so I can whisper."

"Did I go too far?" she asks.

Marcus nods.

"I'm really terribly sorry. It will never, I mean never, happen again. Cross my heart and hope to shit."

Marcus shakes his head. He says, "A lot of these kids don't have your experience, and many people, myself included, feel that that sort of behavior and language belongs outside the classroom, if anywhere. Comprende?"

"These kids?" Kelly snickers. "Grow up. I pass out math tests before rest of class pass out." Kelly rummages around on his desk. She turns around momentarily to scold the few who have gotten noisy again. "Time to clean this desk again. Looks like shit." She yanks a sheet of paper from beneath the elbow of Marcus's still somewhat dead arm. Then she lets out a loud gasp. "You not copy math test. You very naughty boy." She swats him on the arm three times with two fingers held in the boy scout salute. "Very naughty." She goes and copies the problems on the board, or some of them at least. Many she replaces with her own. She is being careful, Marcus notes, to add problems that employ zeroes. She also adds a wider distribution of facts, including the sevens. Marcus never includes sevens. He has hoped for a long time, since he was in fourth grade in fact, that someone would abolish the sevens. He does not wish to put his own students through the trauma he went through trying to learn them.

After writing twenty problems on the board, Kelly turns around to make sure everyone has started. "Everybody work," she scolds. "Mr. Gabriel pay ten dollar every paper one hundred."

"Kelly!" Marcus says.

"Work, work, work. No time play." She copies down the problems in her Barbie notebook and finishes them quickly. She is done in less than two minutes. She writes "ANSWER KEY" on the top of her paper and hands it to Marcus. "Put ten dollar on tab," she says.

Marcus gets out his calculator to check her work.

"Aiiiyeee, him never trust me. Him never learn." She walks up and down the aisles, scolding the cheaters, shaking the nappers. Even though she claims to be twelve Kelly is better than almost all of the student teachers he has had. From somewhere St. Thomas University was always coming up with skittery Scandinavian girls and boys, thin-skinned and easily intimidated types, who at the end of their practicum at Hawthorne announce weepily they have decided to give up their life's dream of becoming a teacher and are going into orders.

Kelly swats someone on the arm. "No peeky," she yells. "Free play outside if everyone finish and quiet." He checks her last problem. Of course they are all correct. She is right. Him never learn.

Butchie Simpson is standing by Marcus's desk. Again. He comes and stands by Marcus every day about this time. Marcus wishes he knew why. Though Butchie is in Tammy's class, he comes to Marcus for math. He has just turned nine, but he is an extremely large child. He doesn't really belong in the sixth grade, but Ione insists he is a boy genius and has forced his age promotion. He is standing by Marcus's desk, leering, Marcus thinks. He is wearing camouflage pants—he is always wearing camouflage pants—and a T-shirt today which has a flag on it and that says "Love it or Leave it."

Marcus stares down at his lesson plans for next week. Maybe if he ignores Butchie, he will go away. Sometimes that works. Kelly has already drawn in his schedule on the planning form. In some boxes—at least a half dozen of them—she has written in things such as: class discussion, ethics and self-governance. Next Wednesday fourth period she has written "learning about yourself and others." These are transparent codes for extra recess and gym time. Mostly, sixth grade was about keeping a lid on things.

When he is at his best Marcus sits on his desk and talks and listens and reads to his students. They like to talk about what went on in their neighborhoods—how many police cars drove through last night, and who had gotten shot or killed; which sixteen-year-old was pregnant for the third time. Marcus recognizes a lot of the names in the stories. He'd sat on this same desk talking to those kids just a few years earlier. They were the same as these kids—scared: about pollution and drugs and nuclear bombs and the fact that there wasn't going to be rain forests any more. Any time a war broke out they were always stunned into silence, numb. They stayed up all night watching and they didn't know what to say. They sat and looked at him and waited for him to talk. He would tell them how when he was in school there was still a Vietnam war, and how he had to—how everyone had to—spend a lot of time figuring out what to do. They knew all about that, a lot of them said. Their dads had gone. Or not gone.

"My daddy went," Leesha said. "He ain't been right since." She had laughed like that was a joke, but no one laughed with her.

"I lived there," said Kelly MaiLee.

He read them books that were much too young for them. Books like *Superfudge* and the Henry and Beezus books. They loved them: sat with their faces open and round, laughing heartily at the silliest parts.

Some days he thinks he just needs to figure out the secret formula, remember the magic words that will ease their pain and lift the pall of sadness that surrounds them, the armor that they hide behind, the facade of aggressive recklessness and wicked high spirits.

And a lot of days he thinks it is just too much to ask of him what they are asking: to tell them how to survive—that it is possible to, or even desirable. He is hip, with it, together, down, chillin, def, phat: the words change, but the idea doesn't. He knows how they see him: he is someone who has jumped into the pool from the highest board, come to the surface, and climbed to the top to do it over and over again. He is here every day, on this desk, with his book and his stories and his legs crossed, listening. He knows that if they never get to the Spanish-American War or to past participles, they will survive. Look at them out there now, giving everything they have to twenty math problems, which elsewhere might be a cakewalk, but here have brows wrinkled and eyes filled with panic. We're trying, those eyes say. Really we are. It breaks his heart that at age eleven, for some of them it is too much to keep their heads off the desks. They are too tired, and it is too hard—it: everything.

The times when he is himself and together—which lately he is not—he sits on this desk, legs crossed and tries to make it look easy. He thinks of the words to one of LaDonna's favorite songs. "Arc of a diver, effortlessly..." those are the only words he remembers. Maybe he makes it look too easy. Maybe he is too cool, but that is the only way he knows to give them hope. They watch him like a hawk, his every move: what he eats, what he wears on his feet, how his fingernails are cut and what comes out of his mouth. They are as hungry as baby chicks. Feed me. Tell me how can I, in the last decade of the century in a cold northern city in a crazy world, hold it together, be calm, whole, reasonably happy?

Like you.

Find a LaDonna, he tries to tell them. In other words. Find the person who is your person, your bridge across the chasm into the light. Find her and keep her by you tight and don't let them take her away from you, because if they do, you will be lost, again.

Like I am.

Butchie is petting at his arm as if it were a fur coat.

"Is there something I can help you with?" Marcus asks.

"Chuz," is Butchie's reply. Butchie can often be found touching Marcus, sometimes fingering a vein in his arm, sometimes picking through his hair the way a chimpanzee grooms its mate. Often he just pets him. Butchie's own hair stands around his head in sharp looking blond spikes. Marcus takes Butchie's hand and places it on the chalk tray.

"I'd prefer it there," he tells him. Though he isn't completely sure, Marcus believes Butchie may be an example of some new kind of genetic mutation. His father, Mitch the park ranger, is a mild-mannered little guy, who reminds Marcus of the cowardly lion—he is even covered all over with blond hair. His mother, Ione, well, she was a Pentecostal lady and one had to see her to believe her. Just yesterday Marcus had told her, "Ione, until you moved next door to me I never really knew what the words built like a brick shithouse meant." Ione, who at the time was waxing the floor in Marcus's kitchen, had blushed and said, "Have mercy Jesus, you just hush your mouth carrying on like that."

Butchie is now making rock and roll lips and tongues in Marcus's direction. He is pursing his lips severely and darting his tongue in and out of his mouth. Marcus does not watch much MTV, but he cannot imagine Butchie is doing this correctly. It looks more like he is having a seizure than anything else. Marcus reaches up and closes Butchie's mouth and presses his lips flat. Butchie continues to rock to whatever music he hears in his head.

People were always telling Marcus that there was something wrong with Butchie. People like Tammy Kartak and particularly his son Ali. Ali spent a lot of time over at Ione's house observing. Every time there is a program about serial killers he predicts that someday that will be Butchie up there on TV. At school, Butchie does most of his assignments, but often does things such as when asked to write a three-page report on the French Revolution, turn in a sociogram of the Tiny Tunes cartoon characters —something that wasn't just off, but way way way off. Very nicely drawn, though, on railroad tagboard with colored pencil. Marcus tested Butchie, himself, on the sly. Had a friend studying graduate psychology give him an I.Q. His friend just shook her head. Can't be done, she'd said. Some people just defied testing. Best she could figure he was either a fifty or a two hundred.

"We don't need no thought control," sings Butchie.

Marcus pats the hand which is still resting in the chalk tray. "Settle down, big fella," he says. At only nine years old Butchie is the tallest child at Hawthorne School. His body is developing rapidly, there are plenty of muscles already strung on his gangly bones. He is the best player—the only good player on the Guns 'n' Roses Trench team. Sometimes he gets made into an honorary brother, especially if one of the Boyz is absent. He bounces off the far wall of the gym to get some good leverage and goes hurtling toward the opposite team like a bull. When he releases the ball he makes a sound like an exploding bomb. When hit, he lies on the floor until dragged away by his feet. He is a whole show unto himself. Someday he might be a good looking young man. He might have to beat them off with a stick, unless, that is, he continues to be as strange as he is right now. Right now his desk is full of G.I. Joes. When the others make fun of him he aims his G.I. Joes guns at them and makes shooting noises. You can tell that as far as he is concerned the bullets have killed them dead.

Marcus cannot understand how two people like Ione and Mitch could have produced a child like this. Sure, he resembles them physically, but Mitch was the sort of person who sat in the middle of the woods and read Wordsworth out loud to himself and the squirrels, and Ione taught bogus courses in Christian literary criticism—was considered a leading authority in the field—prayed intensely before each and every meal, and believed that Butchie had been an honest and true gift from God.

"Hey, teacher, leave them kids alone," Butchie sings. Marcus pats his arm again. The mutation thing: perhaps during her pregnancy Ione was scared by some sort of a satanic horror film, or maybe Mitch had a traumatic experience just before conception that affected his sperm. Something like that might explain a Butchie.

"Where paper?" Kelly gets up in Butchie's face and demands. It is rolled up and sticking obscenely out of the top of his drawstring camouflage pants.

Butchie thrusts his hips forward. "Get it yourself, honey. Have yourself a field day."

Kelly throws the paper to Marcus, shrieks something back to Butchie in Vietnamese that makes the big boys in the back of the room laugh hysterically.

Once again Marcus is sure that there is something about America that many people are missing.

Butchie gets a hundred on the test. He did not even bother copying down the problems.

Mrs. Leighton comes to the door. Behind her Rhonda is sucking luxuriantly on a Tootsie Roll Pop. Mrs. Leighton has discovered that she can get Rhonda up off the cot by feeding her candy from a big dish she keeps on her desk. She keeps the candy on her desk so that students will feel that her office is a nonthreatening place where you can feel safe and loved. Pull the fire alarm, have a knife fight, burn all the *C* paperbacks in the school library: these are among the things students have done with the sole intention of getting to that candy dish. Rhonda is having quite a relationship with her sucker. The juices are sliming out the corners of her mouth. She leans around Mrs. Leighton so that everyone in the room can see that not only has she gotten out of class, she has been rewarded to boot.

"We're having a math test," Marcus says, hoping they will both go away.

"Sixty," Kelly calls. Rusty comes up and gets his paper. Kelly is grading the math tests. As she finishes each paper she calls out the percentage score—thirty-five, fifteen, seventy—and someone comes up to claim it. She does not even need to call the names: everyone knows pretty much who got what. They have all been stuck in the same places since Christmas.

"I'm so pleased to see you staying with the curriculum," Mrs. Leighton says. "It's fine teachers like you that make our school what it is."

Marcus does not know for whose benefit she is saying this. She is always saying things like this to all the teachers, indiscriminately. She says it to crazy Helene, the eighty-five-year-old third grade teacher who has jet black hair like Loretta Lynn and could often be found bolt upright in her chair dozing in front of a roomful of rioting eight-year-olds. She says it to Crenshaw, a fourth grade teacher, who Marcus knows for a fact has used the exact same lesson plans every year for the past fifteen. She says it to Tammy Kartak, who calls children big black baboons.

"Thank you," Marcus says. "We were just getting ready to have a little free time outside after our test. Everybody has worked pretty hard."

"Rhonda says she's ready to join the group now, aren't you sweetie."

Rhonda has an uncanny sixth sense that allows her to determine the exact moment the class was having free time.

"She has not completed her math test," Kelly MaiLee tells Mrs. Leighton. Kelly has converted to her gentle geisha voice. She has also already copied the problems off the board for Rhonda and is sticking them in her face.

"Adults are talking now, Kelly," Mrs. Leighton tells her. Kelly gives Marcus a look that lets him know that Mrs. Leighton will pay for that little remark.

Rhonda sticks a sticky purple tongue out at Kelly. Kelly mumbles something at her, which, though Marcus does not speak Vietnamese, he is fairly sure means something like dirt sucking pot-bellied pig.

"I promise I'll make my test up later," Rhonda says to Marcus. She is back in her flirtatious mode.

"I think that will be fine," Mrs. Leighton says, then whispers to Marcus, "I'd like to chat today during lunch, okay?"

"Fine," says Marcus. Just fine.

Mrs. Leighton leaves Rhonda standing in the door with a look on her face that says "Gotcha." Marcus collapses in the chair which Kelly and Danny have wheeled up behind him.

"You no worry, American friend," Kelly whispers in his ear. "Me you fix boss lady and big hog girl good. Leave to me."

Then Kelly orders the rest of the class out to recess.

"Have a seat," Mrs. Leighton invites. Marcus sits in the same chair which is usually reserved for pugilists, arsonists and other assorted riff-raff. The candy dish on the desk is within easy reach and looks especially inviting. Marcus has not had any lunch. He has no appetite for today's chuckwagon sandwich and tator tots. No one has been able to give him a satisfactory response as to exactly what kind of meat chuckwagon is. In the candy dish are Reese's and Now-and-Laters and Hershey's miniatures. He is not sure what the protocol is when you are called in here. Does one just reach right in or does one wait until their sentence is handed down?

"I'm concerned about you," Mrs. Leighton says. "So I wanted to give you a few minutes of my time." This chair is also the I'm-concerned-about-you-wanted-to-give-you-a-few-minutes-of-my-time chair, or so Marcus has heard. Since Mrs. Leighton arrived two years ago these are the first few minutes he has been offered. "You seem rather down lately," she prompts.

Marcus shrugs his shoulders: give her a taste of her own medicine.

"You're a bit down around the mouth. No energy either."

Marcus half nods and half shrugs. He doesn't want to say anything to her. There is something about this woman he doesn't quite trust. She is simple, always draws the easy conclusion, takes the quick fix. She has thin hair, and wears the kind of women's suits that look like men's suits from the 1960s.

"I understand that your . . . your LaDonna is having some difficulties."

Despite the fact that the story of LaDonna's incarceration was buried on page seven of the Metro section in a tiny article by the obituaries, Tammy Kartak dug it out during her daily combing of the paper to find information to back up her claims about her students' parents and all other people of color. She couldn't wait to bring the copy in to school and share it around the faculty.

"LaDonna takes care of herself," Marcus answers.

And me. And me.

"Well, you know I'm never one to get into someone's personal business. I just want you to know I'm concerned and schools are such a difficult place to work and really require everyone's full energy and attention. You're really valuable to us around here and if there's anything I can do, let me know."

"Thank you," Marcus said. And drop dead and fuck you, too. And, also, bullshit. Schools might be tough, but the last tough day this woman put in was the day she finished her last exam in high school. Marcus had never met a principal in his life he had any respect for. For the most part they were people too stupid, too lazy, or too chickenshit to go into a room full of kids. The old saying was true. Those who can, teach, those who can't, teach teachers, and those with their heads up their asses become principals.

Marcus stood up. "Is there anything else?"

"Actually, yes. Now that I've helped you, I wonder if I could ask you a little favor?"

Again Marcus shrugged.

"Our dear sweet Miss Rhonda . . . " She left Marcus an opening: he knew it was so he could say something unprofessional about Rhonda so that she could write it in her little book and use against him later.

"What about her?" Marcus asks.

"You seem to have some kind of rapport with her. You're one of the few people I think she actually likes."

"And?"

"Well, Tamara's been having a terrible time with her. She won't go to class at all. I'd like to move her to your room."

"Does Tamara know about this?"

"I'm making this decision," was the answer, which meant yes, Tamara did know, yes, she had gone behind Marcus's back, and yes, there wasn't much else to discuss.

"Do whatever you think is best," Marcus said. Out of habit, he went next door to the nurse's station to see if there was a place on the cot. Rhonda was in hers, licking another misbehavior sucker. She gave him a wide evil grin.

"I'm never taking that stinking math test," she says.

He heads upstairs to see if he can find an empty desk in the back of the room that will fit her.

He has made it through to the end of the day. Almost. The sixth graders are outside having recess again. It is hot for April, and the room is stuffy and the kids are cranky and Marcus has barely made it this far himself. So it is okay that they are having another recess. Besides: it is common knowledge among sixth grade teachers that once they start squirming around in their chairs—like they were this afternoon—it is a good idea to head for the doors. Most of the kids are playing kickball. A few are gathered around under the scraggly trees that dot the playground. Marcus is sitting between Kelly MaiLee and Butchie on a low wall that runs along the parking lot. Behind them, Leesha is teasing Kelly's hair into an enormous bouffant.

"Look that Miss Kartak over there think she play kickball."

As usual Kelly is trying to bait Marcus into saying something mean about Tamara. As a diversion he says, "When you talk like that it makes my skin crawl."

She leans around him and says something to Butchie in Vietnamese. Butchie guffaws. He has been playing with Marcus's watch and the wrist it is wrapped around. As best Marcus can remember Butchie was born in Kentucky and should have no idea what Kelly just said.

"Ying, yingyingying Ying, yingyingying Ying," Leesha mocks. Marcus gives her an exasperated look.

Out on the kickball field, Tammy has declared herself all-time pitcher. It is her contention that your average sixth grader is incapable of accurately rolling a rubber ball fifty feet. They only put up with her because they know if they do not she will blow the whistle and make everyone go in and do dictionary spelling words. She draws the ball back and runs up a few steps to release it just as if she were in a bowling alley. Marcus knows that when there are black kids at bat she imagines them tumbling into the gutter.

"Her make me sick," Kelly says crossing her arms.

Marcus bites his lip to keep from agreeing.

Leesha begins a guttural but goofy sounding giggle which means she is about to ask a question. She is so insecure she cannot take anything seriously, not even herself nor anything she is curious about. She is wearing ruby red lipstick that looks especially foolish against her rich black skin. She has ratted Kelly's hair so that it stands at least six inches above her skull. Leesha's hair looks like it is never combed by anyone.

"Can I ask you something," she giggles.

"Go for it," Marcus prompts.

"Some kids said that somebody said that your wife got sent to jail. Is that true?" She collapses in hysterics. Kelly MaiLee drags her away. She leans her against a van in the parking lot and whispers something in her ear.

"LaDonna is coming back," Butchie says. He pets Marcus's hand and pats him reassuringly. "Don't you worry. She will be back soon and everything will be okay."

"Think so?" Marcus asks. Butchie nods. He is looking at Marcus's wrist. He measures around with his thumb and forefinger, then compares that circle to his own.

Everything will be okay. It is such an optimistic thought that Marcus cannot help but smile. That was somehow part of LaDonna's magic. Her ability to make everything okay. And fun. And worthwhile. And alive. He takes out the card from his wallet which he uses to cross off hours the same way some people cross off days. He could just as easily count the minutes. She is in each and every one. It is three o'clock.

"One hundred sixty-seven," he says to Butchie. Butchie smiles and nods. Their hearts beat the seconds.

Leesha returns with Kelly MaiLee .

"Sorry," she says, and Marcus tells her not to worry.

"Everything will be okay. She's coming back soon." Leesha smiles and giggles. She knows. Her dad is in prison, too.

Tamara is dragging a boy named R.J. across the field toward the wall. He is puffing and crying. She is holding him out away from her as if he had lice.

"She better not ever put her hands on me," Kelly MaiLee and Butchie and Leesha say simultaneously.

"Mr. Gabriel," R.J. sputters. He is having crying spasms and can hardly talk. "Every time. (cry-gasp) My turn comes up. (cry-gasp) She. (cry-gasp) Pitches the ball way on the outside. (cry-gasp) Then. (cry-gasp) She says. (cry-gasp) I'm out." Punctuated with a sobbing collapse.

Tamara drops his collar and then wipes her hands with distaste. "If you weren't so uncoordinated you'd have hit every one of those. And when I say you're out you're out, and there's nothing in my contract says I have to listen to back talk from black trash like you."

And Marcus didn't know he was going to say it. He hadn't planned to. It just came out. He stood up and looked Tamara right in the eye and said, "Say what you want about me—I really couldn't care. But if I ever hear you say anything like that again to any of these children, ever again, I will personally kick your butt all the way back to North St. Paul."

Tammy turns around and storms into the door of the school. She is headed directly, Marcus knows, to Mrs. Leighton to tell on him.

Around him the kids stand gape-mouthed. One or two are still holding their breath. Kelly MaiLee says something in Vietnamese which Marcus imagines means, "Holy shit."

"Finish your game," he says to R.J., and off he runs. The rest of them sit back down on the wall. Leesha continues on Kelly's hair, Butchie, fingering the wristband of Marcus's watch. They go on as if nothing has happened.

"We having another math test tomorrow?" Butchie asks.

"I hope not," says Leesha. "I just don't get that multiplying stuff."

Kelly says something encouraging to her in another language.

Marcus remembers the last words to LaDonna's song:

With you my love we're gonna raid the future
With you my love we're gonna seek out the past
We'll hold today to ransom till our quartz clock stops
Until yesterday
Till our quartz clock stops

When Mrs. Leighton calls him into her office tomorrow, he intends to take a big handful of that candy. He will shake his head and shrug and tune out her lecture. Everything will be okay. In one hundred sixty-seven hours, LaDonna will be home.

For now, here, he is surrounded by the strongest people he knows—even if they are worn out, literal-minded and do not know what a four is. They are like rocks, like the four faces carved on the mountain out west. They may be silent but they have seen an awful lot. They have proven themselves brave and fearless and will not let anything happen: to each other, to him, to the whole entire world.

He had promised his son a trip to the Black Hills anyway.

"Which of you guys knows the way to Mount Rushmore?" Marcus asks.

They all point vaguely to the west, in the direction of the sun which is already headed down, already pink out over the cooling prairie air.

From the Diaries of Ione Wilson Simpson, Ph.D.

MARCH 29

Again, Lord, you have blessed us with another beautiful day. A wet snow blew through late last night, but we were greeted with a rosy clear dawn, and though the air was cold, the sun's rays melted away all traces of the storm.

Had two classes today. Almost all students in attendance. Our discussion of *Vanity Fair* did not go over as well as I had hoped. Someone wanted to know why Thackeray would name his book after a magazine. I believe she was serious, but it is hard to say. I pray for these young people feverishly.

We will all need extra strength and resolve to get us through the next few hours. Sister LaDonna's trial is this afternoon. I fear for her. Her impulsiveness will not be an asset in court. I pray that the judge will be patient and forgiving.

Last night: two times. Praise be.

MARCH 30

Another cold and beautiful morning in St. Paul.

The worst has happened: Sister LaDonna has been found guilty. Though I have not been a student of the law I cannot help but wonder if justice has been served. All around us every day people are raping and stealing and snatching purses and killing. Such people get off with a slap on the wrist, if that. Our poor LaDonna has shown horrible bad judgment which has harmed no one. She will be wrenched from the bosom of those who love her and need her. She will be away for almost a month. I will be praying for her earnestly, as I do for us all.

Twice again last night. I am truly blessed.

APRIL 3

Spring has arrived at last in all her glory. Today the sun seemed higher in the sky and there were many birds singing here in the Tangletown area. We all know better than to get our hopes too high. Next week may well bring blizzards and below zero temperatures. We cherish the promise of what is to come.

No classes today. Caught up with the stories and spoke with sister Verda. She is in good spirits today, despite the tragedy that has overcome us all. I have spoken with her about going out to the prison to visit Sister LaDonna, but she says she does not think she will ever be doing that. It is harder on her than it is on the rest of us, but then that is the way it is when you are a parent, or in her case a parent-in-law. We have made a date to have lunch later this week. An afternoon of Christian fellowship can be just the thing to lift one's spirits.

Only once last night, but for a long time. I thought it would never stop. All praise unto God.

APRIL 8

The sky today is the color of newspaper, and now and then there is a sprinkling of snowflakes which sound like salt pinging against the windowpane. I wish it would just snow and be done with.

I did not want to get up for service this morning, but I made myself do so. Though I was tired (and with good reason) there was much to be prayed for. I was sustained by Reverend Miller's fiery, inspired, preaching—today about the satanic influences within the music our youth are listening to. His sermon did just what good preaching is supposed to do: pour a little lead back into your spine.

Back at home my men were lying asleep in front of the big screen television in the basement. I woke them up and fed them tuna fish sandwiches and potato chips. Our Butchie ate three large sandwiches and most of the chips. He is getting bigger everyday. People think he is a teenager, and I have to tell them he is still just a little fellow, barely nine. He is now as tall as me and his daddy.

Mitch spent the afternoon sorting through Butchie's *Ranger Rick* magazines. He is looking for pictures of Minnesota wildlife to paste on a collage for display in the park headquarters. Though most people only come there for picnic permits, he thinks they should be educated and informed.

I fixed a big dinner: I made the Chicken Fajita Oven Enchilada recipe from the *Ladies' Home Journal.* It came out fine, but next time I will use the Velveeta cheese as was recommended.

We all spent the evening lying in front of the TV. I am supposed to be working on an article for *Incarnate Word: The Journal of Christian Literature*, but I am not making any headway on it. My topic is the novels of Jessica Ridgeway McPherson, but I have decided I do not like her all that much. Every time God speaks to someone in her books "it's as if they were struck by lightning," and that is whether they are in the subway or in the United States Senate or in the barn milking the cows. If she plans on continuing to be our finest Christian novelist, she had better come up with a new metaphor of some kind.

Last night five times. Till almost three in the morning. I told Mitch that our marriage was truly blessed.

APRIL 10

Another chilly spring morning, but warm enough to sit on the porch if you stay in the sun. Eight A.M. temperature: forty-nine degrees.

We have had rather an exciting day. I received a call from a Mrs. Something-or-the-other over at the junior high school telling me that my son Ali was in some kind of trouble. That Ali is a little devil, but he is just as cute as he can be, a tall skinny boy the color of butterscotch pudding. As far as I'm concerned he is mine, and I was so anxious I rushed right over to pick up the boy's grandmother. I imagine I gave sister Gabriel quite a fright, and it turns out in my excitement I had forgotten I was still in my curlers and wearing my exercise clothes. (At the time of the call I was riding my exercycle and watching *The Young and the Restless*. I am up to twenty miles a day, which I usually reach before the long break in the middle of the show.)

We rushed over to Hennepin Junior to see what has happened to our poor Ali. Our Ali is not an angel—he has a devilish way about him, can be moody, and has been known to swear and be stubborn—but he is not one to call notice to himself or be sent to the principal. It turns out that after we have rushed all over town there has been some kind of mistake. We talk to a bug-eyed man whose name I do not recall. (Lord forgive me for belittling one of his creations, but I do believe he was the ugliest man I have ever seen.) This man has gathered together any number of African-American youth and put them in some sort of a lineup. Our Ali, of course, is completely innocent of anything, except oversleeping and coming into school late, and that is hardly his fault, seeing how his family is under stress. (I have tried to help out by getting the boy off to school when I can, but many days it is all I can do to get my own Butchie out of here.)

Needless to say, sister Gabriel and I gave this bug-eyed man a piece of our minds, and made him apologize to the boy. Then I took her and the boy back to her house. She had pulled him out of school for the rest of the day.

I had to spend a while in the car reassuring sister Verda. She told me that this was her biggest fear: that something terrible would happen to her son or to her grandson just because of the color of their skin. She said it happens all the time and it could happen to anyone—that innocent black men are shot or beaten by the police or thrown in jail all the time. She told me she didn't know what she should do.

I told her that God loved all of us equally and without question. I said that the best we could do was put it in His hands. She didn't act like it was a very satisfactory answer, and I'm not sure myself that I was helpful. I think I read all these books sometimes because I am looking to find what the right answer is—to this question and to so many others too. Every time you think you've got something figured out, along comes a new wrinkle. The best we can do is put it in His hands. I think that is the meaning of faith.

It is that time again and we have had to stop for a while. (That is why they call it the curse.) Hugs and caresses are almost enough, but not quite. I am praying to the Lord and He is giving me strength.

April 14

Large sloppy raindrops mixed with snow spattered against my windshield on my drive to the Shakopee Women's Detention Center. It is not a bad looking place for a prison, all the same there is nothing inviting about it. The guards processed me through any number of doors before I could get to the visitors' lounge. They do not take anything for granted out there. As far as they were concerned, I was just another common person off the street who would be carrying knives or drugs or something such as that. One woman ran a metal wand up around my hairdo and even poked a finger in it. You best believe I begged her pardon. I had baked LaDonna one of my famous Gooey Butter Cakes—which is one package of yellow cake mix, one package of cream cheese, one package of powdered sugar and a couple of sticks of butter. The guard said we would have to eat it right there in the lounge, which is a shame because this cake is so rich and delicious that you need a while to savor it. Also, it is the kind of cake that only gets better after sitting around for a few days.

LaDonna is looking well, praise the Lord. She says that, all in all, prison is not as bad as it could be. She had thought the other women would be mean and hateful, but mostly they are just sad. Some of them talked tough, but even the loud mouths were basically good people.

I asked her how the food was and she said it wasn't too bad, but there was only so much you could do with government commodities. More than anything she wanted a nice hot slice of pizza.

She said the worst part was having to work every day in the laundry. It was hot there and the meanest guard of them all was the supervisor, and that she spent a lot of her time in the sick room rather than go there. Poor LaDonna. I know laundry is a thorn in her side. If it wasn't for me helping her at home, her folks would be as filthy as pigs.

She told me that a lot of those girls were in a lot worse shape than her. Some were there for a long time, and others never had any visitors. There was one girl next to her room who had hidden her kids from their father, and LaDonna had promised to help her, but she didn't know how yet.

She did all right today, until I told her that Marcus and Ali were fine and they missed her and all. She broke down then and sobbed like a little girl. I held her and rocked her and told her it was going to be all right.

I told her I would come and see her again soon. We left the rest of the cake on the table to be shared—LaDonna said that's the way it worked out there. You had to help each other.

On the way home I was very sad. I cried and I prayed for her to come through this whole and safely. She is a special lady, one who does not always see the world the way the rest of us do. She is an optimist who sees possibility behind every dark cloud. Most and best, she believes in herself, and she is not a quitter. Her schemes may be goofy and many of them blow up in her face, but she is good-hearted and wise, and I believe that on Judgment Day God has a special counter for people like her and she will be able to bargain her way into heaven.

Last night Mitch and I were back in business. I lost all record of time, but dawn was under the draperies towards the end there. I truly thank God for his extraordinary gifts.

April 19

Though I have been disappointed before, I do believe that spring is finally here to stay. The trees are thick with buds, ready to burst. Yesterday where everything was brown, now there is a hint of green, a very pale yellow green.

Our Butchie turns ten today. We had a few of the neighbors in for a little cake and ice cream. Butchie does not have many friends and this is a worry for us. It is because of his size, I know. He is nearly six feet already, and has very big bones. People do not expect a person his size to act like a little boy, but that is all he is yet. He lives inside his head, as well, and does not always know how to make contact with others. This is a phase. I went through it: don't we all? He is a very smart boy, and I'm sure that sometimes what is going on in his own head seems more interesting than anything the rest of us have to say.

Our dear Marcus reports that Butchie is doing well in class. The decision to move him up another grade has apparently been a good one. I am still worried that with his physical maturity, some of those older children will treat him in ways and tell him about things that he is not quite ready for. Lord, there are a lot of wicked influences in the world. I cannot say that I approve of his violent war games and of some of the music he listens to, but I have learned from my own experience that what is denied to you only becomes more alluring. We are still considering a Christian academy of some kind, but there are not as many of those up here as down home, and Mitch is not big on the idea. Also, with both our salaries we still cannot afford a private school. Were it not for Mother Simpson's unfortunate demise, we would still be living in a house trailer. The thought of that makes me shake and reminds me that, despite our familial loss, even in death there are blessings to be counted. I am praying Butchie will find God on his own one of these days. Despite Reverend Miller's remonstrations, I do not believe you can bring a person to God. Certainly not a child. You go to Him or He comes to you. Elsewise, you are not operating from your own faith, but from someone else's. Someday when we celebrate Butchie's birthday, he will be in the church with me. I believe that—for him and for all my other loved ones as well. Until then, I know that God is watching over them and keeping them safe.

For now the best we can do is keep him over at Hawthorne School. I have placed my confidence in Marcus, and I am pleased that he has done a good job with the boy. I know my Butchie is not an easy child to work with. He is sweet with me still, and wants to have a story read to him at night. Were he not so large he would still cuddle in my lap like a kitten.

A festive occasion brings out the tiger in Mitch. He says it is time we moved the boy's room to the basement for more privacy. I try hard to be quiet, but sometimes I just have to make a joyful noise unto the Lord.

APRIL 20

Cold rain all day. Weather that is best forgotten.

Sister Gabriel has gotten herself into another fix. She called me up this evening and she was in quite a state. It seems she has hired herself a maid. Two maids, actually: one for herself and one for Marcus. What she was thinking I'll never know. Being all by herself, she gets a little lost sometimes. I try to look in on her as much as I can.

She says she was trying to do something for Marcus, what with what has happened to our LaDonna. Bless her heart, I know that she has not always seen eye-to-eye with her daughter-in-law. Mother Simpson and I did not always get along either, but we did the best we could because of our love for her son. Sister Gabriel, deep in her heart, knows that LaDonna and Marcus were destined to be together, just like my Mitch and me, and despite the current difficulties, everything will be just fine.

I picked up Sister Gabriel and took her to the Baker's Square so we could discuss her problem. She told me what had happened, how she had this idea about hiring someone to help keep Marcus's home together while LaDonna was away and how she called someone from her church who sent over three girls to interview. She said the first one—a woman called Doris—more or less hired herself to work in Sister Gabriel's house, and then this Doris hired another girl—an Anne Marie—to work at Marcus's house. Sister Gabriel says this Doris is sort of pushy and all of this happened so fast she hardly knew what hit her. Now she says she realizes she probably doesn't need help of any kind—especially if it entails additional shopping on her part—and that though Marcus does need assistance, a thousand dollars a month was out of everyone's reach.

(A thousand dollars a month! Ione, I thought, you have gone into the wrong profession.)

I told her that, in the first place, I, in the spirit of Christian charity, had been doing a fairly decent job keeping Marcus and Ali together, and that when LaDonna was home, between the two of us things stayed in presentable shape, and that secondly, no one kept a cleaner house than she did and to save her money until the time came she needed a hand, and that, finally, as I had told her in the past, she needed to be more firm with people. "No," I told her, is a perfectly good and useful English word, and it never hurt people as much as she might think it did, and even if it did, people were more resilient than she thought and got over rejection quite quickly. We have been working on this for years. One of these days, the Lord willing, she will be less easily taken advantage of, and all of us will rest easier.

I should mention that Sister Gabriel had the French Silk Pie and I had the Sour Cream Raisin. I am learning that you have to be careful with the Sour Cream Raisin: It is a tricky recipe, and sometimes, like today, it can be just a little off. Sister Gabriel reported that the French Silk was, as always, delicious.

Mitch was already asleep when I arrived home. This was quite a dilemma and I prayed for guidance. Then, I heard a voice calling from out in the rain. "Wake him! Wake him!" I did and I am glad I did and the voice proved to have been a voice sent from the Lord. Amen and praise him!

April 23

Glorious spring. The sky is a brilliant shade of blue and the trees are that hysterical early green that they only get for several days of the year. The crab-apple trees are too precious to be believed, with their pink and white flowers dancing in the wind.

Truly there is something in the air this time of year. On campus the girls are as skittish as sweat bees. They break into giggles at the mere mention of anything remotely suggestive, and even the mild-mannered ones are prone to flush and wipe at their brows, legs crossed timidly at the ankles.

In my English literature class we are reading *Wuthering Heights* by Miss Emily Brontë. It is a class of all girls—the boys having given up on words, instead devoting themselves to the diabolical triangle of money, politics and religion. I do believe these books become harder and harder each year for our girls to understand. It is a hard row, with me having to practically read every passage and translate it into what passes for English these days. I found myself in quite a predicament today, explaining one of the numerous scenes of tender intimacy. One can't be too careful how she speaks of such matters. Despite this being a Christian community, there are certain among us who are not above heaping reproach upon a colleague by drawing ridicule upon her pedagogy. I recall last year's incident (cf. Oct. 9) when my esteemed colleague and good friend Dr. Mildred Walker Stevenson was called into the dean of arts and sciences for daring to mention the word evolution to her Science for the Ministry class. 'Twas a snoopy associate in her own department spread the word on her. It is only through the intervention of Jesus Christ Himself she has been able to find suitable Christian employment since, even what with it being editing a journal of questionable quality. So needless to say, I proceeded with caution when discussing the intimate aspects of this novel. (Which I might add I would have hesitated to teach at all had it not been for the state's requiring us to offer a course on nineteenth century literature to maintain our accreditation.)

(As if it were any of the state of Minnesota's business what went on at a Christian institution. Surely their time would be better spent managing the degradation and heathendom that runs rampant throughout many of their public institutions, particularly along fraternity row where such behavior is on display publicly just as if it were a foreign film. All the same we bit the proverbial bullet and as I am the faculty member who has read the most in many literatures, it is I who must deal with the Brontë sisters.)

Today we are working on a section where Cathy meets her Heathcliffe on the moors. I have been trying to get the girls to picture in their minds what these moors must look like. For me the location is rather the whole point of the story. I mean it wouldn't exactly be the same story taking place in the produce section of the Rainbow Foods. But so many of these girls are simple girls who have never lived much beyond their farms out in New Prague, and most of them think of adventure as a trip out to the Rosedale Mall. Having lived only in Kentucky and in Minnesota myself, it is a struggle even for me to picture these moors. So I forgive them their limited imaginations.

We go on to read some of the heaving passion parts. A certain Miss Lisa Anne Wilkerson raises her hand. Miss Lisa Anne is a gum-popping little number from out someplace like Hopkins whose daddy started up one of those evangelical barns with the corrugated roofs and the three thousand-car parking lots. Miss Lisa Anne wears too much make-up and has as her stated career goal to be married to the most successful minister in town. If stories can be believed she is trolling for a certain James Johanssen, one of the stars of the divinity school, who has a silver tongue but is just a little too oily if you ask me. When Miss Lisa Anne raises her hand one knows to expect trouble.

"Yes, Miss Wilkerson," I say.

"Dr. Simpson," she says, all sweet as honey. "Why, with all these heaving breasts and passionate urges, this is nothing but a sex book you got us reading here." All the girls turn red and giggle.

I am momentarily flustered.

Now the point is: this moment would have never happened were I teaching my course in Christian Married Life for Young Women.

For so many of these girls the soon to be discovered intimate aspects of their own married life are an unimaginable idea, as remote to them as those nineteenth century English moors are. Look at them! With their blushing and giggling and sideways remarks. Why most of them think we are talking about hand holding, a snuggle and a little peck on the cheek. They are in for quite a shock, and were it not for the state of Minnesota, they would be somewhat better prepared.

As a Christian educator I feel it is my responsibility to train these young women and prepare them for their duties as wives and mothers. *All their duties.* Tell me, why should they spend these years dreading the unknown, and the first few years of their married lives cowering in embarrassment and shame. A few well-thought-out hints, a little guidance—*some information*, for land's sakes, will open doors these girls can't imagine exist.

Proceeding: Ione Wilson Simpson, Ph.D. is only ever momentarily flustered, and rarely ever that. When Christ opens a door, you walk in—no questions asked.

"Well, Miss Wilkerson," I says. "I do believe you have hit the nail right on the head." And as *Wuthering Heights* is practically required by the state of Minnesota, I proceed to lead our young women through a most lively discussion of the vicissitudes of married intimacy. The girls asked many frank and thoughtful questions—surprisingly not about mechanics so much as wondering if they would like it and was it okay if they did not. I assured them that "it" was a gift from God, meant not only to be enjoyed, but to be celebrated, exalted, reveled in.

(I did not go into details about me and my dear Mitch, though I could tell that they wanted me to. I did not want to intimidate them, nor get their hopes up too high. Not one in a hundred of them will find a man like Mitch. Not one. [Last night . . . well, those Brontë girls couldn't find enough euphemisms between them. Lisa Anne Wilkerson, you should ever be woman enough! {Forgive me, Jesus, and Bless You!}])

The Time I Had to Go to Lunch with a Bunch of Old Ladies, Butchie, and This One Vietnamese Girl

When you are a kid not only does life stink and you don't you have any rights and people treat you like a dog, but then other people get messed up too and it spills over onto you like some sort of contagious disease. None of these people have ever heard the expression "leave me out of it."

So LaDonna is in jail and everybody knows that and Marcus is laying around moping because he says he can't live without her which is the usual thing that happens whenever anything happens to LaDonna. Me: I keep the number of the pizza place handy and make sure the cable TV bill gets paid. *Yo! MTV Raps* ain't free, you know.

My original schedule for today:

1. Sleep real late.
2. Eat.
3. Play some video games.
4. Take a nap.
5. Watch some TV or play some more games.
6. Eat.
7. More games or TV.
8. Sleep.

So I am on my way out the door headed over to Stevie Chatham's house to play Nintendo. The thing about Steve's Nintendo is it is in the basement not right in the middle of the living room and is hooked to a twenty-seven-inch TV in stereo and his mom don't come down there 'cause she's not allowed except to do laundry or something so you can play all day long and not have to worry about being hassled. It's not that he has more games or anything 'cause he don't.

My first mistake was I stayed in bed too late. I blame that on Marcus who was he a normal parent would have made me get up and do something constructive like make the bed or wash the toilet, but Marcus is not only not normal, on top of that he is in bed having some sort of breakdown. It was a bad week at work. Some shit went down, but all I get out of him is a bunch of sighs and telling me to please leave the lights out. Last night Ione sends over Butchie with a batch of monster cookies and this round bumpy cake with a hole in the center and with white gunk all over it. Butchie and me, we ate all that shit ourselves. Butchie is a big old dude and a mental too. He will eat anything even all the weird shit his mom makes. Marcus, he don't need that kind of crap. When you are depressed what you need to do is to have people leave you the hell alone. After we ate, I kicked Butchie in the behind and told him to get his white ass out of my house. It's okay: he likes that kind of stuff. As I said, he is a sick mental.

I open the door to go to Steve's and there is Grandma Verda. "Oh, Baby," she says, and throws her arms around me. You would think someone has died, except Grandma Verda is a crazy old lady and you never can tell with her.

"Well, get him and let's go," Ione says.

They grab me by the arms and throw me in the back of the car with Butchie before I can say anything.

"We should try something new some time," Verda says.

"You can get a perfectly lovely meal at the Baker's Square," Ione says. Ione zooms the car around the curb, almost on two wheels it goes. She drives like a maniac.

Butchie is rocking his head back and forth and strumming up and down on an imaginary guitar. He don't even have headphones on. I look over at him and he mouths the word "Yeah!" I mouth back the word "retard."

"I just thought we might want to try some place new. One of those nice places on Grand Avenue. It was just a thought I had."

"Now, Sister Gabriel: you know you love that French Silk Pie. And anyways, you told them to meet us at the Baker's Square. Aren't the boys behaving themselves nicely? You boys sure are behaving yourselves nicely back there."

Butchie doesn't say anything because he now has some sort of solo for which he has to concentrate hard and contort his face and run his fingers up and down the neck of the guitar. He jerks off the guitar in my direction and I kick his big butt and tell him to stay over on his side of the car. If I'd known I was going to be kidnapped like this I'd've brought my Walkman and a comic.

"I should've asked Doris where she likes to go. I bet she might've known about a couple of new places."

"It's too late to waste our energy on things that can't be changed. You can have the Patty Melt. You like a Patty Melt. And just keep your mind on that French Silk pie. Mm Mm Mm." She speeds through a red light. Her big old car roars like a lion.

"You sit up back there, Ali," Verda says. "Lord why don't these children think more about their posture. Just what I don't need is a grandchild all bent over like a hunchback."

"It's a blessing this child has a grandmother like you to look out for him. Tell your grandma how lucky you are," Ione orders.

"Whatever," I say.

"Isn't he a precious. And just look how full this parking lot is! What do you think all these people are out here for on a Saturday morning anyway?" She zips into a space which it is obvious some other people were waiting on.

"I hope we don't have to wait for a table," Verda says. "We may have to go some place else. I hear that Lee's Kitchen is nice."

"Keep your mind on that pie, sister."

Ione tells me to mind Butchie while she goes up and gets us on the list for a table. Butchie gets a big perverted grin on his face when he hears this. Mind Butchie. Butchie is taller than me and has about thirty-five pounds on me. Well, he is only ten, and you never know when one of these Highland Park dudes might go try and steal an enormous retarded-looking kid. So I tell him to sit down by me on the red bench. He practically sits on top of me and continues rocking. I shove him away, punch him in the arm and tell him to try and act normal. He rubs his arm and does a goofy laugh.

Ione is up at the counter with Verda, strong-arming the host into giving her the big booth in the non-smoking section. This will work because the host is a man today and Ione has her enormous tits stuck in his face and is lecturing him. The host tells her the booth is reserved but he can put her in the smoking section, but she says absolutely not will she have her clothes and hair ruined by all that nasty cigarette smoke and that she has been a regular customer for going on fifteen years as have many of her friends and on and on about how she has never been so insulted and if he knew what was good for him he'd show her to her table right now because she was not afraid to go over his head and then he'd really be sorry. Verda stands there the whole time with her purse hooked over her arm and her mean scowl on her face and I guess between the two of them and Ione's enormous tits it is more than he can handle because before you know it he is showing us to a table. We get real nasty looks from a bunch of folks in the lobby who were probably waiting for that table themselves. Think Ione cares?

We walk across the restaurant and everyone stares at us like they ain't never seen a fancy looking black lady, a mental, a relatively normal youth and a lady with big boobs and a lot of hair piled on top of her head.

"Take a picture: It'll last longer," I say .

"Get in, get in," Ione says when we get to the booth.

"I thought there were six in this party," the host says. You can tell he is not happy.

"The other two will be here momentarily," Ione says. "And you can have your girl bring me and sister Gabriel here a cup of your delicious coffee and bring these boys here a couple of large Cokes. Get in, get in," she says.

She makes Butchie and me slide around to the middle of the booth and then she hops in next to Butchie and Verda next to me. Verda puts her arm up around me.

"Cozy," Verda says.

Verda sighs. "Nothing on this menu appeals to me today."

"Have the Patty Melt, sister. You know you love the Patty Melt."

"Well . . . that does look good. I was thinking today I would try something a little different. What do you recommend?"

"Personally I am having the club sandwich. You can never go wrong with a club sandwich. But, you go on and have the Patty Melt, sister."

"Well, I don't know. What are you boys having?"

Butchie is having some sort of a fit trying to play peek-a-boo with me from behind his menu. Every time his big head pops out he twangs a guitar chord. When no one is looking I reach in there and grab his ear and pinch it as hard as I can. He howls like a rock star.

"You boys behave," Ione orders. Butchie puts down his menu and sits up real tall in the booth with a goofy grin on his face.

"Can I have two burgers, mama?" he asks.

"Let's just see here, baby," she says. "He's so hard to keep filled up these days," she says to the rest of us, then cuddles up with Butchie to pick through the menu.

"What about us?" Verda says to me. I can tell she wants a little boy to cuddle and pick through the menu with, too.

"You should have the Patty Melt, Verda" I say.

"Think so?" she says. And then she says, "Doris! Doris!" real loud and starts waving and making everyone in the place look at us.

Here comes this lady I never seen before. Behind her is Verda's crazy neighbor, Marjorie and that Vietnamese girl who lives at her house.

"You all got here at the same time," Ione says. "And looky here is my precious Kelly. We're just gonna have to squeeze in a little more and make room. Butchie, you say hello to Kelly, sweetie."

Butchie sticks out his tongue real nasty-like. Everybody pushes together toward me. I am practically crushed, what with Butchie on one side and Verda on the other. Grandma drapes her arm further around my shoulder and Butchie starts feeling on the back of my knee. I use my finger with the longest nail and dig it into his arm.

"Ahh," he says, with a big smile.

I told you he was a sick mental. I decide against giving the same treatment to Grandma. If I behave she may give me some money or something.

"Everybody cozy," Ione says. She has made introductions all around. Even the people she don't know she has introduced. "Isn't this a lovely luncheon us all here together? Now let's all decide real quick before our little waitress comes back. I'm having the club sandwich."

Everyone opens their menus up. While they are busy Kelly tears off one end of her straw wrapper and blasts the rest of it across the table at Butchie. Butchie sticks his middle finger up his nose, digs it around and flicks it in her direction. I may be the only normal person at this table, except there is that one old lady Doris who I don't know.

"I can never make up my mind," Verda says to this Doris.

"Well I can't help you 'cause I don't ever come to this place," Doris says, and Verda gives Ione one of her grandma looks—the I-told-you-so look, the one she is always giving Marcus whenever something bad happens to LaDonna.

"Everything is delicious," Ione says, ignoring Verda. "Especially the pies. Tell her about the French Silk, Sister Gabriel."

"It's lovely," grandma says. "Just lovely."

"Hmmm . . ." this Doris says.

"Mother," Kelly asks. "Would it be all right if I just had a salad?"

"Is she not the most polite thing?" Ione gushes. "How old are you now, sugar?"

"Twelve."

"Oh! She's getting to be a big girl," Ione says.

Kelly's all snuggled up with her mommy and looks as sweet as sugar. Don't believe it. Every Saturday morning she runs a crap game in the alley behind Verda's: dollar in, nickel bet. She keeps trying to get my eye, but I won't look at her.

"Waitress! Waitress!" Ione calls. "Someone is looking at a short tip," she tells us. The waitress, who is spittin' mad, brings the rest of our waters and takes our orders. I order the Works Burger, which has everything on it, and Verda orders the Patty Melt, and the rest of them order a bunch of other crap. The waitress snatches our menus and leaves.

"Someone will be getting a letter in her file," Ione says, and then she says. "Well, here we all are."

"That your grandbaby?" Doris asks about me. She's one of them round black ladies with a face looks like she might hit you if you got smart with her.

"Yes, this is my Ali," grandma says.

"He the one whose mama . . ." Doris says, and raises her eyebrows real suspiciously, like I wouldn't know they been talking about LaDonna. Verda closes her eyes, sighs and pounds her chest.

"And you're the nice lady who'll be helping Sister Gabriel with her housework," Ione says.

"Uh huh," Doris says, like it was none of Ione's business.

"Bless your heart," Ione says, and then grandma sits up and starts clearing her throat, and even I can see there's gonna be trouble.

A piece of ice hits me in the forehead. "What the . . ."

"Shshsh." Kelly has her finger over her lips. "Meet me at the bathrooms in two and two," she mouths, and then she says, "Mother, may I be excused to go to the lavatory, please."

Marjorie, who has just been sitting there writing in her notebook, says. "Of course, darling." I bet she's been writing down every word's been said.

"Excuse me, everyone," Kelly says, and slithers out the booth after her mom gets up to let her out.

"Isn't she precious," Ione says.

"I think we should get down to business," Marjorie says.

Grandma flinches and Ione swallows.

"Business?" Doris asks. "This some kind of meeting?"

"Well, actually," Ione says, and stills Butchie, who has been blowing bubbles into his Coke. "Can I call you Sister Carter?"

"You can call me Doris."

"Doris, call me Marjorie, and the thing Ione and I are concerned about is this housekeeping deal you've got set up with Verda."

"Concerned, are you?"

"Thank you Sister Peterson for being so direct. Yes, we are concerned, what with her living on a fixed income and all."

"Looks like she fixed pretty well to me."

"Look, Doris. We neighbors look out for each other, and it seems to me . . ."

"It seems to me that you all are meddling with the affairs of a grown woman."

Grandma is holding on to me so tight I can't breathe. She's staring straight ahead in sort of a trance. Later for this, I think, and announce that I got to pee too, ooze out onto the floor of the booth and crawl out between all the legs. Butchie tries to follow me, but Ione tells him to set. She probably needs him to protect her for the big standoff. Thank God, too, cause I don't need to be in the bathroom with that big pervert.

Kelly snags me and pulls me into the little phone alcove where the bathrooms are. "What took you so long? I been standing her five minutes."

I shrug.

"Nice jeans," she says. She grabs a belt loop and spins me around and starts looking around my butt for the label."

"Guess. I like those. How much you pay. Forty? Fifty?"

"LaDonna got 'em."

"How much she pay? You can tell me."

"How'm I supposed to know that?"

"They fire that black lady yet? Marjorie says they're gonna let her have it right here in the restaurant. Think I want to sit there and watch some shit like that?"

"I think that was what was going on when I . . ."

"Don't you hate my outfit. I look like fuckin Cindy Brady or somebody. Yesterday I saw me the cutest outfit in the Limited. A black leather skirt up to here and a striped blouse and a biker jacket. Boy, it was tough. Guess how much. Three fifty. When my Social Security comes I'm getting me that bad girl."

A man in a one of those little Jewish hats squeezes by us. Kelly pushes right up against me and mumbles something in Vietnamese. I can feel her little titties against my chest.

"You go to Hennepin, right? You like it there?"

"That school sucks."

"You know this one guy Demetrius? He's like, okay, he's darker than you, and shorter, you know him? We used to go out. Yeah, well he kind a dogged on me, and shoot, I didn't feel like putting up with his shit so I dropped him."

"I think our food is coming," I say.

"Marjorie, she don't like me going out with the brothers, but she don't say that because she don't want nobody to think she's prejudiced. I figure, shit, what she don't know won't hurt her. Right?"

A fat lady pushes past us into the women's bathroom. Kelly rubs up against me and this time she puts her hand on my butt.

"We better get back," I say.

"You and me, we need to talk," she says. "When you coming over to your grandma's again?"

"Come on," I say. She pushes her hair back behind her ears and leads us back to the booth.

"I'm a business woman with expenses like everyone else," Doris says.

"And I'm sure you do a wonderful job, Sister."

"I done told this woman about patronizing me."

"All right, enough," Marjorie says, and she gives me and Kelly a look like we were up to something. Butchie makes shame fingers and gives us a big grin. "Let's just go over the details and make sure this is settled. Verda agrees to pay fifty dollars a week for weekly cleaning service. Is that correct?"

"That's what we agreed to," Ione says.

"Why you can't let a grown woman speak for herself?"

"Doris," Marjorie barrels on. "You'll take the fifty and not solicit Verda for any more."

"If that's what she wants."

The waitress looks like she can't believe what she's hearing. She slams the plates down any which way, asks if anybody wants anything else. We all ignore her.

"And finally Ione, you'll call that agency and cancel that other housekeeper."

"My pleasure."

"Now, maybe we can have a pleasant lunch," Marjorie says. She closes her notebook and gives me what I think is a dirty look.

"Grace before we eat," Ione says. "Join hands."

Verda gets one hand, and on the other side Butchie grabs my other. His hand is damp and sticky and disgusting.

"Precious Lord," Ione begins. Her head is bent over and her big hair floats out over her sandwich like a balloon. "It is our true privilege to be gathered together in loving fellowship in your name. We thank you for the many blessings with which we have been bestowed: for our loved ones, our good health, this bountiful meal we are about to receive."

Butchie begins sliming his hand around mine so it feels like I am holding some disgusting animal. "Knock it off," I whisper.

"We pray for those who aren't with us today. We pray you will watch over us all and keep us in your loving care."

"This food's getting cold," Doris says.

"We pray all this in the name of your son, Jesus Christ. Amen."

Kelly says the loudest "Amen" of them all.

It takes us a couple a minutes to trade plates around. That waitress didn't get anybody's right. Butchie tries to play sneaky fingers with my french fries, but I jab him a couple of times with my fork so he stops.

"Here, honey," Ione says, and scrapes all hers off her plate onto his.

Every now and then Kelly catches my eye and mouths "Call me. Don't forget." Marjorie is like she's trying to catch me looking at her.

The nasty waitress comes by and starts clearing plates. "Who wants pie?" she asks.

"Everyone wants pie," Ione answers. The waitress rolls her eyes.

While she's gone to get her pad, Marjorie gets everyone's order on a page of her notebook. She even draws a picture of who gets what and where.

"This ought to make it easy for you," she says to the girl, and then she and Ione exchange smartass looks.

Verda's first bite of pie. She looks like she's died and gone to heaven. I'm glad she's enjoying it, 'cause I guess that it's been a rough time she's been having.

"Good pie, huh, grandma?" I ask her. I'm having the banana cream.

She just lets out a big happy sigh and gives me a hug.

Mitch

The black squirrel that lives on the south side of the lake has lost more of his tail. I believe he has a nest in the rotted out knot of the ancient elm tree. Scrappy little fellow: he will take on almost anything. He's getting up in the years, too, and I am surprised he is still with us.

The last crystals of ice washed up on the eastern shore of the lake last week. Duck sex is the order of the day, and I expect many more little ones this year than last. The weather has favored us and there has been corn and bread all winter long. We are all well-fed and happy. A half-dozen bachelor ducks bicker and sulk and gorge themselves over by the main parking lot of the lake. Take heart, men! Summer is soon. Soon I will be searching the bushes and underbrush for nesting. Most will survive, and some will fly off elsewhere, but many will stay, and you will have many new mates to woo next spring. It amazes me that here, by this lake, in this park, in this city, life renews itself so basically and so well.

A mallard with a busted wing stumbles from beneath the lilacs. Feathers helter-skelter, he is weak and slow and I am able to gather him in a tarp and carry him across the footbridge to the office. He is docile and I soothe him and feed him Ione's homemade wheat bread. We call the vet and I continue my rounds.

Over by the wolf woods a rare pileated woodpecker has been spotted, and in the thicket just to the south of the picnic grounds I uncover a most intricate network of chipmunk holes—a regular subdivision. A white feral cat lives here also, and I hope she does not eat too many of their young. The wolf woods are Butchie's favorite spot here. Butchie, my son, my big old boy.

In the lake itself there are turtles, turtles, turtles, and this, for me is a good sign. We are trying to save this lake, rerouting the storm sewers which contain all the motor oil and road salt and dog shit people wash down there. For five springs now I've sat here, the first warm day that the ice is out and there is sun and it is warm and watched for the turtles to emerge. So far I have not been disappointed, and I wonder how I will feel the day they do not emerge. I wonder if we can even stop that day from coming.

The vet says there is nothing to do for our mallard. He is put down and is left for me to deal with, and though it is not the policy, I find a spot near the chipmunk colony, dig deep, and place him there, wrapped in the tarp. I read this:

Form is the woods: the beast,
a bobcat padding through red sumac,
the pheasant in brake or goldenrod
that he stalks—both rise to the flush,
the brief low flutter and catch the air;
and trees, rich green, the moving of boughs

and the separate leaf, yield
to conclusions they do not care about
or watch—the dead, frayed bird,
the beautiful plumage,
the spoor of feathers
and slight, pink bones.

That is by Jim Harrison, a man I would very much like to meet.

Toward evening, the air cools and the park quiets, save the unearthly screams of the peacocks who live in the Japanese garden. It is five. Another day of hope and death. I wash the soil from my hands, scrape my shoes, and head on home again to Ione.

The Black Hills

"Hey, you know what would be a good thing: if some of these little fuckers around here had to pick up for themselves," Tony says. Tony is the part-time night custodian at Hawthorne Elementary. Presently he is running a wide rag mop between the desks and Marcus is filing student papers into the waste basket. The papers are this week's spelling assignments: copy the word three times and use it in a sentence. After seven months he has reached an understanding with his students: They would prefer he dump the papers directly and save them the trip. This afternoon Tony is more full of grouse than usual. "Looks like a goddamn toilet in here," he says.

"We do our best," Marcus says, though he isn't sure that's true. He does sort of try to get his sixth graders to pick up at the end of the day and they do sort of attempt to. Mostly, by three when the buses finally come, everyone, himself included, is too exhausted to do much more than drag themselves home. Playing school for six and a half hours was more work than most people imagined.

"One thing my old man did was make sure we picked up our own mess," Tony says. "I couldn't get away with half the shit these little fuckers do." Tony always works in something about his old man. Marcus listens politely and nods his head. That is part of the unspoken deal: the kids get to leave a mess and Marcus gets to listen to Tony. First, Tony complains about how filthy Marcus's room is. Then Tony tells how the Buick Regal is running and what he plans to fix, replace, tune up or rotate. Then Tony complains about Dawn, his trashy girlfriend, who Tony is convinced is sleeping with all his best friends and who every time he threatens to leave her announces she is pregnant with his kid but always turns out to have only been late or had some kind of tumor. Next Tony complains about his father, that asshole, who is a drunk and a deadbeat and who, if he didn't need a place to stay he would "kick his drunken butt back to Bemidji," and as soon as he saved enough to get his own place he will beat the fucker up to pay him back for all the times he beat him up when he was little. Their session ends with Tony laying across the reading table looking forward to the day he gets his mechanic's license and then can quit this piece of shit job and really get on with his life. Marcus says things like "Really?" and "Is that a fact?" and "What happened next?" He thinks of this as therapy, for him and for Tony. For Tony because for the most part after high school no one ever listens to young men like him again except for maybe other young men like him—other young men who also have beat up old cars and trashy girlfriends and abusive dads—and for Marcus, because it reminds him that most of his students probably will survive and maybe become decent sorts of fellows—like this Tony. Look at him: despite it all, he was still doggedly optimistic, believed someday things would work out for him. And, also, for Marcus it was good because it reminded him that, all things considered, his own life wasn't so bad.

Tony has swept most of the garbage into a single mound. He is wearing a sleeveless Motley Crüe shirt. It is the same shirt many of Marcus's students wear. He gets up and helps Tony realign the desks in neat rows. That is another part of their unspoken deal.

"I see you're skipping the big party downstairs," Tony says. "I swear to God, every time I look up, that one lady teacher got herself knocked up again."

"You should be down there yourself," Marcus says.

"They don't invite me to that shit. That's for you big shots around here. Me, I ain't shit."

Down in the first floor teacher's lounge, the faculty is celebrating the fact that one of Hawthorne Elementary's first grade teachers, Mary Sue Nelson, is having another baby. Marcus cannot remember if this is Mary Sue's fourth or fifth or sixth baby, in fact he cannot remember a time in the past seven years since she came to Hawthorne when she wasn't either pregnant or on maternity leave. When he is napping on the nurse's office cot Marcus overhears enough office gossip to know that Mary Sue and her husband are trying for a boy. Mrs. Hooks, the secretary, keeps telling people that maybe this time they will get lucky—as if being pregnant were some sort of roulette game and having four or five healthy girls wasn't already some kind of luck. Marcus hopes they get that boy—because Mary Sue is a nice woman and people should get what they want—and he also hopes that years of adult therapy will someday help those girls get over this.

Marcus is skipping the shower. No one at Hawthorne Elementary is speaking to him right now except for his sixth graders and Tony. The teachers are angry because Marcus has told off his teammate, Tamara Kartak, and though a lot of them feel, deep in their hearts, that Tammy deserved being told off, especially considering she is divisive and hateful and a racist and a snob, this telling people off business was the sort of behavior that, if left unchecked, could get out of hand. Rather than risk being put in the position of being confronted by anyone about his or her own shortcomings, the rest of the staff has gathered round the wounded chick and hung the giant A around Marcus's neck and are avoiding him as if that A stood for AIDS.

"Heard you told that Kartak broad off," Tony says. "I can't stand her myself. She talks to me like I was her fucking slave. 'Carry this to my car for me.' 'Empty that trash can.' I'm gonna bust her in her fucking lip one of these days."

Marcus doesn't respond. All he needed at this point was to have been in a conversation with a custodian about Tamara.

"Nice tits on her though," Tony adds. He has emptied both trash cans now and is making himself a place to lay down on the reading table for his afternoon break. "What exactly did you say to the broad?"

"Just spoke my mind," Marcus says.

Abusively: that was the way Mrs. Leighton characterized his mind speaking. And, *she* simply could *not tolerate* having someone on *her staff* who felt it was all right to speak to others in an *abusive fashion*. She asked to hear his side of the story, and he told her. He told her that Tamara had called one of her students black trash and that if she ever did something like that in front of him again, she'd regret it. He didn't tell her that he'd threatened to kick her butt, figured she'd already heard that part and it didn't need any more rehashing. He had popped another Hershey's miniature in his mouth—a Krackle. He'd grabbed a big handful out of the bowl Mrs. Leighton kept on her desk. She kept them there so students would feel welcome and not threatened. He had creamed the chocolate with his tongue and tried to figure out if that's how he felt.

Past caring: That was how he really felt.

"You should have come to me," Mrs. Leighton had said. "You put yourself in jeopardy by doing what you did. Vigilantism doesn't get us anywhere."

Because she had his fate in her hands, Marcus felt it was undiplomatic to remind her he had gone to her in the past—about this and other things—and, that her lack of follow-through, skill, conviction, backbone, morality, common sense, and decency was exactly the reason this country needed vigilantes. People were just plain sick of the bullshit. He chose to say nothing.

"I'm giving you a verbal warning. This time," she said. She tried to be stern, and there was something in her tone—some nasty guilt-mongering you-owe-me-one catch in her voice—that made Marcus feel beholden. He hated feeling beholden. This was the same verbal warning that everyone got, including Monique Gomez, a fifteen-year-old fifth grader who had pulled a knife on the bus driver, and Jeremy Hilton, the kid who had burned all the *C* paperbacks from the library in the trash can of the boy's lavatory. And then they got offered candy, so they knew there were no hard feelings. Marcus had already eaten half the bowl. As far as he was concerned there were plenty of hard feelings.

"Anything else you'd like to say?" Mrs. Leighton prompted.

Marcus never had anything to say to her, really. Deep down, she probably wasn't a bad person. In her heart she just believed that people were basically good and deserved a second chance, and that the world was a hard place which sometimes caused people to do things they didn't mean to do. Like pulling knives on people, burning books, and telling off racist bitches.

Marcus believed all that, too: who didn't?. But he also believed that there were lines. He didn't decide where they were: They were generally agreed to by everyone. Things such as: You picked up after yourself. You didn't bother other people's things. You made amends. You didn't do hurtful things to kids—the way Tammy did. It was all right to *think* mean thoughts—like he thought about the giant cow of a sixth-grader, Rhonda. (He liked to imagined Rhonda trussed up on a platter, surrounded by tropical fruit and with an apple stuck in her fat mouth.) Sure, it was okay to think those things, but the line was: you never said them or did them. Or at least decent people didn't.

He knew some people who liked living right up against the limits —liked dancing on the line—and he had to admit that for him it was thrilling to watch those fools. It was one of the reasons he loved these kids, and one of the reasons he loved LaDonna, too. People like them went as close to the edge as they could, got as close as they could to the fire, close enough to feel its searing heat. And when they got too close sometimes they got burned, and maybe they learned something from it and maybe they didn't. In real life that meant you went to jail sometimes. As LaDonna had done, and maybe she'd learned from that just how far she could go with her little schemes. And maybe she hadn't.

At Hawthorne when you got burned it meant that the fire got moved and you stuck your hand in again and again, and what you learned was that there were no limits and you were invincible, and it was a lesson that served you pretty well.

Until you were shot in the back running out of a convenience store with forty-three dollars of loose change dripping from your fist. The problem with Mrs. Leighton was not her compassion—if that is what it was—but the fact that the rest of the world didn't operate that way. In the rest of the world, NO generally always meant NO.

"I do have something else," Marcus had said, plucking a miniature Mr. Goodbar from the bowl and popping it in his mouth. "There's a family emergency we have. A relative—an aunt. She probably won't make it. She's in South Dakota. I'd like to go out and see her one last time. In the morning if I could."

Of course, she'd said, of course. She would even arrange for the sub for Thursday and Friday. That's the kind of decent person she was.

So Marcus is not at the shower because he is at his desk preparing lesson plans for two days.

Marcus doesn't have an aunt in South Dakota. To the best of his knowledge he has only one aunt, in Michigan, and several uncles, two on his father's side. They are all robust and healthy.

"I'll be gone for a couple days," he tells Tony. "Think you can handle it here without me?"

"Shit, if you're leaving, I'm leaving too. You're the only one keeps these little assholes in line around here."

"Give them your broom. Put them to work."

"That's exactly what I say. Best thing for 'em," Tony is reclined on a nest of reading papers, hands behind his head. "You hittin the road?" he asks.

"Me and my boy," Marcus answers.

"This ain't your vacation, you know."

"No, Tony man, but sometimes you just gotta go." He closes his plan book and gives Tony the high five on the way to the Bronco.

He has had enough. He cannot face another day, not until she returns. All the pettiness and pressure and bullshit and garbage and crap. It is like the giant oil spill in Alaska: it is simply unmanageable anymore and things will get ruined and it will only get worse. It is time to walk away and just let it be for now.

It will all be easier when she gets home.

He is taking his boy and going to the Black Hills for a few days.

LaDonna is coming home soon. In one hundred fifteen hours.

Ali has been clicking up and down the dial on the radio for the past forty minutes. There is a blast of news and then there is a blast of Garth Brooks and then there is a blast of farm reports and then there is another blast of Garth Brooks.

"Jesus. They don't even have anything on the radio out here."

"You shouldn't take the Lord's name in vain," Marcus says. Exactly what his mother would have said.

"Who?" is Ali's response. Marcus realizes they have neglected the boy's spiritual education, but he didn't think it was this bad.

They are driving west on I-90, twenty-some-odd miles from a place called Windom. This radio thing is a bad sign, Marcus thinks. As best he can remember, there is no big, real place that might have a decent radio station between here and . . . Well, maybe Minneapolis is like the last place. As best he can remember, if you keep driving on this road you drive right into the Pacific Ocean, only it takes you a couple of days and you probably won't see any people.

Marcus does not mention this to Ali. It is too dark to read and Ali is hungry and cranky. Were he to find out it was Garth Brooks and farm reports between here and forever, he might get out of the car and walk back to civilization. Right now he is sitting with his seat tilted back and his feet resting on the dash. If Marcus runs into something Ali will be decapitated and the rest of his body will fly through the windshield like a rocket. He is at that adolescent stage where suddenly there seems to be more limbs than there is boy to carry them around.

"Are we gonna stop, or what," he whines.

It is almost seven-thirty P.M. and they have been driving since four.

"Down the road here a piece," Marcus answers.

"What is this? You get out in the country and all the sudden you start talking like you're from Mississippi or something."

"We'll stop in Sioux Falls. I promise."

"Sioux Falls, Sioux City, Sioux Sewer. Where do they come up with the names for these dumps?"

"They have a contest," Marcus says. "Whenever somebody finds a new place, they have this contest where they ask people to send in suggestions for names. Then the committee votes and chooses which is the best entry."

"Really?" Ali asks. Seriously, he asks it. Marcus can't believe how gullible children are. How gullible and obnoxiously curious. They were always asking questions about stuff you could never imagine, never prepare for. Stuff like: How do they get those cats to dance and sing in the cat food commercials? What exactly is a transmission, anyway? Why, if you could see on the TV that there was the president giving a speech, where was he and how could you tell that was really him? And you could essentially give them any answer you liked, even though most of the time you didn't really know what the answer was nor completely understand the question, for that matter. You could get away with any answer but "I don't know." Somehow, "I don't know" had become the rudest thing a person could say.

"The truth is: a lot of times they name places after the people who lived there," Marcus answers. "Sioux Falls for the Sioux nation."

"Cool," Ali says.

When they get to Sioux Falls there are restaurants clustered around each of the exits.

"Get off here," Ali orders.

Marcus directs the Bronco toward a cluster of bright signage. He follows Ali's pointed finger into the lot at Burger King. Ali orders a Whopper for himself and a chicken sandwich for Marcus. Marcus claims that the menus in fast food restaurants and the teen-age girls who take your order incapacitate him.

"Is there a 'no kids' section?" Marcus asks. Apparently not. The restaurant is filled with young families, each with more children than can be managed by two adults. Everywhere there are loud voices, and giggling and bickering over snatched french fries. They find a mostly clean booth by the front window, slide a tray full of mess to the side, and sit down. Ali tears the wrapper off his sandwich and takes two huge bites. He hunkers over it as if he expects someone to snatch it. Marcus gives him a disgusted look, but he goes right on hording. A french fry sails over Marcus's shoulder from some urchin in the next booth.

Ali picks it up, dips it in catsup and sails it back.

"Hey!" the mother of the kids yells.

"Get your tubes tied!" Ali yells back.

Marcus holds up the time out sign. He leans over and whispers for Ali to chill out.

Marcus figures he better eat. He takes the top off his sandwich to see what it is. You can never be too sure. He recognizes the meat as chicken. It is even an irregularly shaped piece of meat like you would make at home, but he is disturbed by the dark stripes across it.

"What do you suppose those are?" he asks Ali.

"It's charco-broiling. Duh—don't you know nothing."

"Anything. This looks like it was painted on. This looks like someone took a brush and painted stripes on it. Do you suppose it's okay to eat this?"

Ali grabs a pack of catsup, slathers it all over the meat and slaps the bun back on it. He shoves it in Marcus's direction. "What you can't see won't hurt you. Eat, for God's sake. You get thinner every day. You better eat before Verda puts you in the hospital or something."

Marcus takes a bite from the sandwich. It is dry and chewy and reminds him of chicken when LaDonna makes it, which makes him sad and he sighs. He is a hopeless wreck. Even his own kid sees through him now. He puts his head in his hands, elbows propped on the plastic booth. "I'm sorry," he sighs. "I've made a mess, haven't I? I'm sorry."

Ali sticks a wad of napkins in his father's face. "Just eat your chicken sandwich."

"Reminds me of her," he mumbles.

"That bad?"

"I don't even know what I'm doing any more. Where are we? Some place in South Dakota at some restaurant? What kind of life is this for a kid? I'm ruining everything."

"Finish your sandwich, Dad."

"Why do I even pretend to take care of you? Of anybody? I can't even take care of myself. You'd be better off at Mom's. I'm taking you back to Verda's."

"Sit down, for God's sakes. People are looking at us. Finish your food."

"People are looking at us, they're thinking: that guy is a loser and a terrible father. That's what they think. And you know what? They're right. It's decided. I'm giving you to your grandma. It's for the best."

"You know what I hate? When LaDonna goes off on one of her deals and you feel sorry for yourself and start to go crazy and act weird. Look at my watch. Thursday. She's coming home Monday. Four days."

"Monday. Four days."

"Yes, Monday. Now: Eat your food. You promised me a trip to Mount Rushmore, and it's too late to turn around."

Marcus takes another small bite from the sandwich. It is cold now and tasteless, and reminds him even more of LaDonna's home-cooked meals. He holds the bite in his mouth a long time before washing it down with the Coke.

"And don't even think you're gonna get away with dumping me at Verda's. I'll sue you. Kids are doing it all the time these days."

Marcus nods.

"She's fuckin nuts, your mother is. Sits around all day long watching TV and doing crazy shit. Anybody tell you your mother was nuts?"

Marcus nods.

"Are your done with your whining? Are you back to normal now?"

"I think so."

"Good."

"Good."

"We better check the map," Marcus orders.

"We're headed west is all that matters. Let's just roll." Ali scoops all garbage from the table onto his plastic tray. He wedges open a trash container and shakes most of the leavings inside. He leaves the tray hanging out the opening.

Marcus reaches to fix things, but Ali bats his hands away. "They got people to do that," he says.

They swagger out to the Bronco, loosening their belts and kicking gravel.

"Get your tubes tied?" Marcus asks.

It is past twilight and the sky is black, starless and without any depth at all. The highway goes straight ahead, rolling through gently undulating countryside. The inside of the Bronco is a dimly lit cocoon, and Marcus cannot imagine what the land is like beyond the windows. He is traveling through a place he has never seen.

They have settled for country. Despite himself Marcus finds he likes many of the songs. So many brave and resilient souls, and melodies that are surprisingly catchy and tuneful. A song about a man who prays every night that if he dies someone will feed his dog. Lots of good drinking songs. Right now Marcus wishes he were a drinking man. He wishes he were one of these good old boys, drunk, sunk under the weight of it all, nothing left but the bottle for a buddy.

Ali is stretched out across the front compartment, legs sprawled at painful looking angles. His head has rolled over near Marcus: he is warm and breathing in a way that Marcus knows means he is mostly asleep.

Marcus imagines the landscape here as sylvan: the interstate lined with tall trees as a windbreak. He knows that isn't true. The road rolls rhythmically beneath the wheels. They are the only car out here. He imagines this is a wonderful place to live. He would like to live here with her.

He remembers her hair, how it swirls and blows around her head when they go riding together on open empty roads like this one. How she hangs her head from the window the way dogs do, feeling the air on her face. How she says it feels to her the same way flying must feel—as if the air were a solid thing your body sliced through, as if you were nothing and everything at the same time.

There she is standing by the road, waving for him to stop. And there she is again. The Bronco spits gravel behind it as it weaves off and onto the shoulder. Ali wakes up with a start.

"What the fuck?"

"I guess I'm getting tired. I guess we should stop for a while."

"Whatever." Ali snuggles back down to his sleeping posture.

Marcus drives ten miles to the next rest area.

They are waked at dawn by pounding at the windows.

"Hello, hello," the voices say. There is one on each side of the car.

"Ohmygod . . ." Marcus says, startled.

Ali sits up and grabs for his father. In the dew distorted windows their faces look demonic.

"Anybody home?" one window asks.

"Hello?" asks the other.

Sleep addled, Marcus is beyond rational. There's a thought roaming somewhere something about safety. He powers down the window about two inches.

"Something we can do for you?" he asks.

"Hi," the one at his window says. She is young—sixteen, maybe—a skinny girl with blond hair that recently had been feathered out from her head in tiers—the way they all wear it lately—but now mostly hung limp and straight to her shoulders. "I'm Ellen," she says. "And that's Stephanie."

"It's Ellen and Stephanie," Marcus says to Ali.

"What do they want?" Ali says, and yawns and stretches as much as he is able, splayed out across the small back compartment. Stephanie, a heavy set girl who looks like she might be an Indian, wipes the dew from the back window to get a look at Ali. She cups her hands around her eyes, the better to see in with.

"What seems to be the problem, Ellen?"

"You can roll down your window. We don't bite or anything, do we Steph?"

The darker girl doesn't respond. She is scowling, too busy trying to get a fix on what is sprawled across the back seat.

"Dad . . ." Ali warns.

Marcus powers down the window halfway.

"Hi. I'm Ellen and that there is Stephanie and we have a bit of a problem. See last night after I got off from work—I work over at the Trucker's Home, up at exit 310—you know that place?—you don't? —so I was off at eleven and my boyfriend, Cletus, he picked us up—me and Stephanie, that is, 'cause she had come by to meet me 'cause we was all going over to a party in Stickney. You know where that is? You don't? So we get there and the party was out on the county road, out in somebody's barn.

You know how they have those big parties out in somebody's barn? Sometimes they're fun and sometimes . . . Yeah and well it was so hot in there you wouldn't believe it—I liked to died in there, got all sweated out in my arms, and I hadn't planned on washing this uniform till tomorrow. This is my work blouse, by the way, 'cause I was working swing shift last night and there wasn't time to go home and change, but you know I figured there'd be a lot of people there just come as they are, so what the hell. Anyway, to make a long story short, I stepped outside to cool off for few minutes and next thing I know here comes Stephanie to tell me to come on back inside 'cause there's trouble. I come back in and Cletus was squared off with this one dude from down there some place who I had never seen before except he looked sort of familiar. That being unusual for me seeing as how I know pretty much everybody in this part of the state, what with it being so few people and all. Cletus, he's a circling this guy and mumbling at him. They was about to have World War III in there. See the thing about Cletus is, he's usually real sweet unless he gets to drinking—which fortunately for most everybody is not too often. We been going together for—what is it, two years almost now? I don't know how serious we are or anything. I mean, I guess I could do worse, you know. I mean, he's been to trade school and all—he's a welder—and he's talking about moving up to Aberdeen 'cause he's got family up there and all and he figures he can get a job in construction or in an auto body shop or something. Me, I'm thinking, Aberdeen, well shit. I mean its not like that's the big city or anything, you know what I'm saying? I'm thinking what the fuck am I gonna be doing in Aberdeen. Not that there's any reason to stay around here. In the middle of fucking nowhere. It's just me and my mom out here. She works over at the co-op in Chamberlain. Jesus, she's worked there so long it's a wonder she don't own the place. My dad, he split before I was born, and I mean, come on, can you blame him? Take a look around here. And I don't want you to get the impression that Cletus is bad news or anything, 'cause considering what you got to choose from around here . . ."

"They're black," Stephanie says, still staring in at Ali.

"Duh!" Ellen mocks. "You got to ignore her. She ain't quite right. Got dropped on her head or something. Indians!" She waves her hand as if to dismiss the whole race.

"Start the car and let's go," Ali says through his teeth.

"That your boy back there? Hi! He favors you, don't he? People say I look like my daddy, too, but I wouldn't know, seeing as how he took off and all. He's probably the reason I got these skinny legs. Cletus, he says these legs are so damn skinny, one of these days he's gonna pull them apart and make a wish."

"Start. The. Car."

"It was wonderful meeting you, Ellen."

"Hang on just a second. So, it turns out, I get there just in time to break up this big fight, and I get Cletus out of there and we head on back out to Pukwana, and me, I'm so relieved that we didn't get our butts kicked that I don't notice that apparently Cletus had had more than a few cups of beer and he was a weaving and a bobbing all over the road, and it was just about here we picked up the police and they took old Clete on in and left me and Stephanie out here with the car. Turns out Cletus, he took the keys right on to jail with him, which is probably just as well, seeing as how he don't allow no one—not even me, to whom he is practically engaged—to drive. And so here me and Stephanie are: obliged to depend on the kindness of strangers, such as yourself. Where are you good people from?"

"Start the car, give her a quarter, say good-bye and get the hell out of here."

"St. Paul. We're from St. Paul."

"St. Paul! Do you know a Bambi Bergeron? Well, actually, I don't know if she goes by Bergeron or what. I think she lives up by where . . . there's a big Monkey Wards store there isn't there? Stephanie has a bunch of folks there too, but you wouldn't know them. I mean, they're Indians and all."

"We don't know any Bambis or Indians and it was nice meeting you good-bye start the car dad. NOW!" The Indian girl is still staring at him and making his skin crawl.

"It was very nice meeting you," Marcus says. "My son and I are gonna head out. Is there anything we can do for you before we go?" He turns over the engine.

"See, Stephanie. Did I say . . . What I said to her was over in that Bronco I bet are just the nicest gentleman who will help us in our time of need. You see the thing is—Stephanie: run over and make sure all the doors on Clete's Chev are locked—the thing is, here we are at this damn rest stop. No one knows where the fuck we are. Pocohantas over there leaves home last night as usual without a nickel, and me, like a dope, I give Clete all my cash so he can take care of things down at the jail. I figured, he'd be out by now if he was coming, but, I mean, this is like his twelve thousandth DWI, you'd think the guy would learn. Either that or the asshole was so drunk he forgot where the hell he left us. So, what we was wondering, Stephanie and me, was could you ride us into this little town down here? It's not out of your way or anything. Three exits down. Twenty-five miles. Thirty max."

"Say 'no'," Ali hisses.

"Pretty please?"

Marcus rolls his eyes. "Oh, what the hell." He pops the locks open. "Get in."

Ali has put on his Walkman and is sitting as far over on the backseat as is possible. He looks straight ahead of him, trying to ignore Stephanie who is still staring at him. He is afraid she is going to spit on him, or at least that's what her expression tells him.

"I can eat all the chocolate I want and my skin never breaks out," Ellen says. "Really, it's true. This one time I ate a whole bag of those Hershey's miniatures and didn't get nary a blister. Well, actually I didn't eat those dark chocolate ones. I can't stand those, can you? I gave all those to my dog, Muffin. She's a Cockapoo. She threw 'em up all over my mama's white chenille bedspread. Don't you know mama had a fit. Yes, she did. I bought her a new one though. They had them on special at the five-and-dime. Fifteen-ninety-nine, I think I paid for it. It's a lot nicer than the one she had anyway. Muffin is so precious. If I had my purse, I'd show you her picture. She's my little angel, she is. Y'all got any pets? Stephanie, stop staring at the boy back there. Is she bothering you, honey? She ain't right. I told you that, didn't I? I swear, you can't take her anywhere. But she's my friend and so . . ." Ellen shrugs.

"No pets," Marcus says. He is watching the road signs more diligently than usual. The mile markers seem farther apart out here:

Although he is going well over seventy, it seems to take minutes to go a mile.

The sun is up behind him and he can see that the land around him now is open and rolling and brown. There is nothing to see, save billboards for the casinos in Deadwood. In the daylight this girl is younger than he thought, younger than she pretends. She is so white her skin appears almost blue and transparent, blotched a bit at one corner of her mouth with a bit of acne or crust of some kind. She is spindly as a stick person, all her flesh eaten by the nervous energy her whole body twitches with.

"Shit, I wish I had me a cigarette. None of y'all smoke, do you? Stephanie, you sure you ain't got no more cigarettes? Hell, I guess it's best I quit, anyway. They say it ain't good for you, but you know I figure you gonna die, you gonna die. We had some colored at our school once. Actually, it was just one boy, and I think he was really only half. See, what I heard was his mom she run away down to the cities and while she was there she got mixed up with one of them and that's where he come from. He was real nice and he got along real well with everyone. It was almost like he wasn't colored. What y'all do down there?"

"You mean my job? I'm a teacher."

"No shit! I would have never figured that. I mean, I never knew they had any that was . . . well, you know what I mean. Man, I hated school. Never learned a damn thing."

"She's a dropout," Stephanie says.

"You're not even in this conversation. And I told you to stop staring at that boy. Dumb bitch. She's the one dropped out first anyway. At least I got a job. All she does is sit on her ass all day, eat Doritos and watch soap operas."

"You might need that diploma someday," Marcus encourages.

"Yeah, yeah, no lectures, okay. So one of these days I'll get a GED, right. Like this school shit is so hard, I mean you add up a couple of numbers read a few paragraphs and they give you a Ph.D., I mean, so fucking what. Here I'll be living in Aberdeen dropping some welders kids every year. You need some damn diploma to do that? Do you?"

"Education is about a lot . . ."

"Holy shit, Steph, did you see that? Over going the other way that was Clete's brother, Ray Junior in their dad's pickup. Asshole's probably coming out to get us. He'll shit a brick, he drove all the way out there for nothing. Okay, take this exit and go left under the overpass."

The exit has come up out of nowhere, barely marked, undistinguished. The town is a wide main street that looks as if it has been placed here intentionally, like a movie set or a theme park. It is a grain elevator and a few stores only, clustered south of the exit, away from a tiny new motel and gas station complex. A few cars are angle parked in front of a cafe. There is no other traffic.

"Stop right here," Ellen says, and Marcus angles the Bronco in front of a plywood-covered storefront with a wooden porch.

"It's been real," Ellen says. "Thank y'all so much, and y'all drive safe, now." Both girls hop out and take off running around the building. Stephanie stops to turn and wave good-bye.

Marcus backs the Bronco into the street and drives to the corner. Around behind, the backs of the buildings face open fields. There is no sign of anyone at all. "Where do you suppose they went?" he asks.

Ali sulks, slumped into the seat next to Marcus. Marcus has asked him if he wants to stop at Wall Drug or the Reptile Gardens or at the Mystery Spot or at a half dozen other tourist traps. The only response he has gotten is silence. Ali is not speaking to him. Again. It was a teen-age thing. Sometimes they became deaf and mute like this. Could last hours or weeks. Marcus believes he himself did not talk to his own mother, Verda, for at least a year at one point. He can't remember why, but is sure it was over something important like socks or green beans.

"I guess I get to make all the decisions, then," Marcus says. From his years in sixth grade, Marcus knows that the mature and appropriate response is to not feed into this at all and to just ignore Ali, but then he was sick of being mature and appropriate, and it was his car, goddammit, and he hadn't driven all the way across America to be ignored. They came out here to have fun, and they were gonna have fun.

"I heard that there is a great museum here in Rapid City. It's supposedly the best museum of Plains culture in the country. I can spend the whole day in those places."

Ali sneers and sputters through his lips. He locks his arms tighter across his chest and puts his head back. Marcus knows this is the part where he is supposed to swerve the car off the road, slam on the brakes, grab the little prick by the collar and ask him what gives. And Ali would then have a crying fit and confess what was wrong and Marcus would give a manly speech about values and priorities and Ali would feel better and thank him and they'd hug and get on with the trip and live happily ever after. But this was not television and there was no script writer to make it all turn out neat and pretty. It might end horribly, just down the road here, in a terrible crash, or not end at all, go on and on, just like this for a long long time.

"Straight to the mountain, then, I guess," he says, and still there is no reply.

They head out US 16 and then onto the winding road into the park. Everything is eerily familiar here—there is a strong sense of déjà vu, but there is no specific memory associated with any of it. Marcus thinks of *Gunsmoke* but he isn't sure why. They park the Bronco, skip the visitors' center and go right out to the viewing area.

"There it is," Marcus announces. It is a foolish thing to say, because of course there it is, otherwise why would they all be out there looking at it, but he feels the need to say something to his son, because he is the father and this is his trip and, after all: there it is.

"Isn't it bigger than that?" Ali asks.

"What do you mean?" Marcus responds, conflicted, because though he doesn't want to be having a stupid conversation such as this one, he does want to be communicating with his child, and then, also he thinks, that, yes, it does seem a bit small.

"I mean that when you see pictures of it in real life it seems like it's a lot bigger than that."

"This is real life. And, I know what you mean."

"Maybe it's bigger up closer."

"There's trails down there. We can walk some. You want to walk?"

"Nah."

"Me neither."

So they sit on the wall and look at it some more. Clusters of tourists come and go around them. Some, like them, seem rather sad and disappointed. The ones with babies hold them up and pose for pictures and point to the mountain and say "see" and Marcus wonders what it is the babies see. Trees? The blue sky? A white thing that looks vaguely like faces?

"Why'd you let those girls in our car?" Ali asks.

"I don't know. It seemed like the right thing to do."

They sit some more. Dangle their feet over the wall. Marcus sees some birds he thinks may be hawks. Or eagles. He is a city boy. How's he supposed to know what the stupid things are? He just knows they seem graceful and important, as if they owned all of this themselves.

"I wish we hadn't run into them," Ali says.

"Well, we did. Sorry."

And for only a second Marcus wonders what he is sorry for. Sorry he stopped? Sorry he was kind? Sorry, really, he thinks that this is what it's like here in real life, and it's not giant post card size and perfect, and also sorry because, like the bumper sticker says "shit happens"—most of the time boring shit and strange shit—and there wasn't a thing to be done about it. And, as a father and a teacher and an adult and therefore one of those who feels he should help make this all different and better and wonderful and perfect, he feels the need to go on and apologize for all of it, and he concocts his spiel and is all ready to deliver it, until Ali says,

"Okay." Just okay, and then. "Who's that other guy up there anyway?" and Marcus is off the hook, relieved, and he looks up and sees them looking somewhat the way they did in an old history book when he was in fifth grade at J.J. Hill School.

"Let's see: there's Washington, Lincoln, Jefferson—like on the coin—on the end there, and the other one in between is Roosevelt. Teddy," and he thinks, of course Ali wouldn't know this, since this picture and theirs have been purged from the history books, and now are featured only on television, mostly on cartoons where they talk and they sing and—like everything else on TV—are larger than life and not quite the same.

"And people drive from all over the country for this," Ali laughs. "Now, Dad: you have to admit that this is some pretty strange shit. This is a weird world we live in."

Pretty strange, Marcus agrees, and weirder than you can even imagine. And he has an odd sense of relief that, with an attitude like this, somehow, maybe his son might be okay.

"Just look, I mean, a big mountain with some dead guys carved on it, and all these assholes out here looking at it."

"Including you and me," Marcus adds, patting him on the back. "Ready to go? Leave now we should get in Saturday night in time for bed. Sunday morning we go get your mom."

They head back to the interstate and turn east. Marcus promises not to stop for anyone or to pick up anything along the way except for fast food. It's a promise he hopes he is able to keep. Ali keeps looking out the back of the car as if they have left something behind.

"Hey, you know what I really don't get," he asks. "If those were the Black Hills, then where were all the black people?"

Marcus just keeps his eyes on the road and keeps on driving.

Sunday Dinner

MARCUS AND ALI

It is Sunday again and the weather is warm again and everyone is out driving again, this time along Highway 13, headed toward Shakopee. Today is some big deal at the casino and Marcus and Ali, who are on their way to the Shakopee Women's Detention Center, are stuck in a traffic jam full of fools.

"These assholes," Ali says. "Be better to just flush the money down the toilet."

Marcus has given up chiding Ali for his filthy mouth. He has no idea where Ali's unfortunate predilection has comes from: not anyone they know curses with any regularity or even very well: not himself or LaDonna or Verda or Ione or anyone. The only person Marcus remembers who had a mouth this foul was his father, and he has been dead for over twenty-five years. Maybe it is a genetic thing, like brown eyes or buck teeth.

"Look at this asshole," Ali says. Marcus looks over at the car they are creeping past on the left. Inside is a Lutheran type and his wife. They have put on their Polo shirts and visors and are off for a fun-filled day of low-stakes blackjack and video slots. Ali waves and gets the guy's attention. The guy smiles back, and Ali makes a jerking off motion with his left hand. Fortunately the left lane opens up and Marcus can make a fast get away.

"Lose your shirt," Ali yells as they speed away.

"You're going to get us shot one of these days," Marcus warns.

Ali waves his hand at Marcus, dismissing him. He goes back to drumming on the dashboard. From somewhere he has gotten a pair of old drumsticks. The plastic tips on them are nicked and rough looking. He is drumming along to a rap tape. The music repeats itself in a way that causes Marcus to zone out on it, but now and then he catches a phrase: many of the words he doesn't believe are actually English words, and some of the words that he does recognize give him a start.

"Excuse me," Marcus says, "did I just hear something about throwing whores out of bed?"

Ali shrugs. "It's 'hos,' and it's just an expression," he says.

Marcus pushes the eject button and tosses the tape out the window beneath an eighteen-wheeler.

Ali continues drumming. He hasn't missed a beat. "Plenty more where that came from," he says.

Marcus cuts over into the left lane to go around a car towing a boat trailer. He then cuts back to the right. The casino traffic is starting to back up for the left turn. Though he is missing cars by inches, he does all this maneuvering smoothly and calmly and only gets a few honks from the other drivers. They know a pro when they see one.

"It's just that, I wouldn't want your mother to hear that sort of thing. It degrades women, if you know what I mean."

"Doesn't bother me. You owe Butchie ten bucks, though."

"That was Butchie Simpson's tape? You could have told me before I dumped it," Marcus glides around a stalled car using the shoulder. There's a clear shot ahead for about a mile, as long as nobody from the left lane tries any funny business. He leans on his horn and floors it.

"Butchie's tape?" he says. "You know what I don't get. If Ione is so religious and all and Mitch is like this big nature lover, where did they get this kid? He's so . . . He's . . ."

"A sadistic perverted Nazi retard," Ali says. "Those the words you're looking for?"

"Actually, no," Marcus says. "And he's certainly no retard. He happens to be my best math student, but all that aside: I just don't get what's up with this kid."

Ali drums on Marcus's head. "Wake up!" he orders. "You ain't figured out the story over there next door yet?"

Marcus shakes his head.

"Stay tuned," Ali says.

Marcus thinks that just maybe he will. Now that things would be getting back to normal and everything.

NEXT STEPS

"Hold out your hands," LaDonna says. Nancy does and Officer Resnik does and LaDonna smears them each with a dab of white cream.

"Tingly," says Nancy.

"Refreshing," says Officer Resnik.

"And doesn't it smell yummy? Go ahead," she prompts. Both women wave their hands in front of their noses, close their eyes and inhale. They open their eyes dreamily and each begins massaging the cream into their hands.

"And guess what the best part is. Look at me and guess. Oh, never mind. See my skin, how radiant I am. I slept in it last night. It works, it really really works. We're gonna be rich." LaDonna waves the jar of cream around, doing a little jig. She stows it in the bag she is packing.

"You are something else," Officer Resnik says. She backs toward the door of LaDonna's tiny room. "You take care out there. Don't want to see you back, you hear?"

"Thanks for everything, Shultzie."

Officer Resnik rolls her eyes and waves good-bye.

Nancy, sitting cross-legged on the bed, watches LaDonna pack the last of her things. "What will I do without you?" she says. But she doesn't cry. They are way past that now.

"Just stick with the plan, girlfriend. We'll have you back with those kids before you know it."

"Gosh, LaDonna, what if *60 Minutes* really does come? Can you imagine? Me on national TV?"

"You sound like you have doubts. Never, and let me emphasize never, underestimate a Madame LaDonna plan. By the time we're through there's not a judge in this country will be able to deny you."

Nancy comes over and embraces her. "Even if . . . no I'm not doubting . . . Even if all that happens is I wrote some letters, at least I don't feel so helpless any more. I have you to thank."

"When 60 *Minutes* comes, make sure they send that fine Ed Bradley. You know, the black dude. Wear your hair back," LaDonna flips Nancy's hair behind her ears. "Like this. Just a little foundation and some pale green shadow. We want you looking pitiful but not pathetic."

Nancy starts snivelling.

"What's this, young lady! Shall we review step ten?"

"Shoulders back."

"Shoulders back."

"Chin out."

"Chin out."

"Forward into the light."

"Forward into the light."

They march down the corridor, arms around each other, toward the security desk.

From the Diaries of Ione Wilson Simpson, Ph.D

April 29

From spring to summer. The temperature this morning is already sixty-two degrees and we have opened all the windows for the first time to let in the glorious fresh air. Some cardinals have taken up residence out back, I believe somewhere around the tall old oak. That mama is so fussy today that I had to put on a hairnet to drop a paper sack in the alley trash bin. I believe she and I will have to reach some understanding about just whose yard this is. Out front my Mitch and my Butchie are throwing a ball back and forth in the spring sunshine. They are like two blond angels.

Well the day has arrived at last. Our LaDonna is coming home. I wanted to go to the prison to welcome her back to the world, but thought, no, that should be a family time. Let them be the first ones she sees. This has truly been a difficult month for those who love her. Surely He had a purpose for giving us this trial, and we will all be stronger and better because of it. Now is the time for each of us to reflect and to come to understand what we may have learned.

For me it is how we have been strong together and have been pulled closer, this little family we have here. And maybe more than anything, I have learned that that is what we are: a family, though not in the way most people talk about it. There is a big, dangerous, lonely world out there and we are fortunate to have found each other. We had best cling unto each other like those biblical tribes of the Old Testament.

Sister Gabriel is having us all over to supper tonight. She has been cooking for days and will put on her usual delicious spread. It is her way of celebration, of making peace and of bringing us all together. I am bringing dip and my famous pretzel salad, which is more of a dessert than a salad. It is the one you make with the Cool Whip and cream cheese and pretzels. Wouldn't you know the store was out of blueberries. I have had to resort to a strawberry topping for it. We shall cross our fingers and think good thoughts.

Last night with Mitch was an extra blessing, a true turning point, a message from on high. I don't know what it was—we did not do anything unusual or different or special—but I was . . . transported is the closest word I can call. I was floated above the world, and where I came to was, is, an . . . understanding. I still float now even as I write.

God has revealed His purpose: I have been called to lay forth a true pathway to transcendence. My daily blessing is to be a blessing for all. It has fallen to me to spread the word.

God gives us the call but not always the path. It is for me to determine the best way to spread His news. Whether it is through books, pictures or a combination thereof, I don't know, and I must be prepared to be scorned and ridiculed, to be painted with the same brush as the pornographers and smutmongers. So be it. I am strong. I have been chosen, and He will guide my hand the way He has guided my dear Mitch all these years.

Hallelujah: I am born again. Again.

Me and my big mouth again

Well, Miss crazy lady Verda is having a big dinner party, and I must be losing my mind because here I am over here helping out. As if I didn't have anything better to do with my time but come over and cook for half the folks in St. Paul. And for free, no less. She's a crafty one. First she calls me up and tells me she's gonna have a few people over and do I think I could come and that I was welcome to bring my husband and all that. As if I could get his lazy butt up from in front of the ball game on a Sunday afternoon. Not even if they was givin away free money down at the First National Bank. Then she gets to sighing and clicking her tongue and talking about how she can't remember the last time she had so many people over her house and she didn't know if she had the strength. That's what she kept saying. Don't know if I have the strength. 'Bout twelve times she says that. Well I ought of let her big hint fall over dead on the floor like the pile of doo doo it was, and ordinarily I'd've given the bitch a good piece of my mind, but she caught me one of the times I was feeling happy and enjoying life, and I said I guess I could come over and help her get stuff set out. Do me a favor: slap me next time you catch me in one of those moods.

I get over here about one, and wouldn't you know it she got everything pretty much done. All the food is on and the table's all laid out and the house is all clean. So she takes to second-guessing herself. Oh, Doris, she says, do you think I should put out some different candy and are these candles the right color and do I think she had cooked enough potatoes, until finally I have to bring her into her living room and tell her she better get herself cooled down before she blows a fuse. I tell her that even if she didn't do another thing she have outdone herself already and that if any of these niggers or white folks she got coming over here wasn't satisfied, to hell with 'em. I told her until that roast come out of the oven she wasn't doing one other thing except sit down here with her shoes off and enjoy the Lord's day. I told her to get us two glasses of tea and that me and her was gonna have us a nice visit.

So, we're talking about this one and that one, and I tell you that this a lady love to gossip. Turns out even though we travel in a different crowd we know some of the same people. And her husband, the one that died, well he was related to them Gabriels that lived up off of Lexington before they put the freeway through there, and her brother-in-law was the one used to run around with that Geraldine Hughes live over on the next block from me. And, I'm fixing to fill her in on the latest on this Geraldine when in walks that hippy woman neighbor of hers from the turquoise house. In addition to needing a haircut . . . naw, Doris, don't start in on folks on the Lord's day.

Well, this hippy gal, she got a whole bushel basket full of all kinds of green stuff and she calls herself gonna make a salad. She says she got some arugabugala and some endust, and I'm thinking she be better off just getting some cabbage and tomatoes and forget about all this carrying on. Not as if Verda ain't cooked enough food as it is.

Remind me to pick through real careful when we get to the salad part of the meal.

A REGULAR LINDA GREGG

RETURN OF THE MAIDEN
by Marjorie Hanks Peterson
(for LaDonna)

As the goddess kisses the somnambular ground
Piercing her fertile loins
Awakening
The dormant life-stuff whose
Tender tendrils reach, ache
Yearn for the warmth of the new spring sun,
So, you return to us, now,
Fair and wise woman/child
Your presence
Golden promise of
August in a stillborn
Still winter night

Plastic-slip-cover-city

By the time we get to Grandma's everyone else is already there. Kelly and her mom and that Doris and Ione and Mitch and that crazy pervert retard Butchie. I go on inside, but LaDonna and Marcus stay in the car. They probably have some more loving and stuff to take care of before the big party starts. The first thing of course is to get past all the slobbering and stuff from Grandma and Ione, Ione who says oh just look how big he's getting and tall and so handsome and making a big fuss—as if I'd been out of town for two years and she hadn't just seen me this morning before we got in the car to go get LaDonna. So the best thing you can do when her and grandma get going with the slobbering and carrying on is just go limp and stand there until you can go to the bathroom and wash all the slobber off. By the time they're through and what with LaDonna and all her carrying on I am practically soaking in it.

There is food everywhere and still Grandma and this Doris and Verda and Kelly's mom are hauling it in and setting it on the table. There is dip and stuff on the coffee table and Mitch and Kelly and Butchie are shoveling it in like it is the last meal before they get shot. I elbow my way in there to get my share. Kelly says something to me in some other language, and she and Butchie just laugh. I give them the finger and start grubbing.

"Isn't that good?" Ione says. "It's real simple. Just cream cheese covered with Heinz chili sauce mixed with shrimp."

Is she talking to me?

Every Sunday at 4:00 p.m.

Verda can see them out there in the car from behind the drapes. Sitting out there, just sitting, bigger than life, for the whole neighborhood to see. Sitting there, practically in his lap. That dumb awful woman. Just look at them. If they were decent people . . . but, ha! Why even talk about decent. Just look at her. You'd think she was coming home from winning the Miss America pageant instead of coming home from prison. Everyone on the block—hell, everyone in St. Paul knows where she's been, and a normal person might not want to advertise the fact, might think to be driven to the alley entrance, through which she ought to enter anyway, seeing as how all she is anyway is an alley cat, but her, no she has to come right in front, right where everyone can see, and, where all these nosy hags up and down the block are ready and waiting with their camcorders. A normal person would have some compunction. But her? Shameless. That's what she is.

And forget about the fact that there are all these people in here waiting on you. And all this food I've been up all night slaving over a hot stove to prepare, and now it's going cold, because we're just sitting here like we was on a cruise and this was the all day buffet. Don't give anyone else a thought but yourself. The heifer.

I'll fix her, Verda thinks. I'll fix her good, and for a moment she regrets not hiring Anne Marie, not hiring the little trollop to set this wench out on the curb once and for all. But only for a moment she thinks this, because she knows that really that plan was too simple, had too many holes. There were too many ways it might fail. There has to be some way. She has to think of something. Something. Anything!

Then a big smile crosses Verda's face. She chuckles.

"Are you all right, Sister Gabriel? They coming in yet?"

"Call everyone to supper, Sister. We'll be eating shortly."

"Bless you," Ione says.

"And bless you, too, honey." Verda hugs her around the waist. Yes, bless us all, everyone, she thinks. Let's just think of this as a new round, shall we. One of these days, oh yes. One of these days. She'd get her. She'd get her, and she'd be gotten good, once and for all and forever. One of these days . . .

. . . I NEED MY LOVE TO TRANSLATE

"You miss me?" she says, finally. They have been sitting, forever, silent, together.

He nods.

They sit some more.

"I missed you, too," she says. They sit. Hold hands.

He nods toward the house. She shrugs. Arms around each other they head for the door. The house is wide open, and there they all are, everyone they know and love, gathered 'round that big table, a table as full of food as always. His mother stands, waiting at the head of the table.

Marcus presents LaDonna, with a flourish of his hand, wordlessly, like the prize models do on *The Price is Right.*

Ione cups her hand over her mouth, and her tears stream over her fingers.

"I love you all," LaDonna says, and blows a big kiss around the room. Verda smiles her smile and turns her head to catch the kiss, or so it might seem.